THAT BOY

THE ALL AMERICAN BOY SERIES

REMY BLAKE

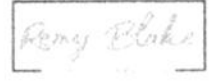

Cover design by JustWrite.Creations
Edited and Proofed by Shauna Stevenson at Ink Machine Editing

This book contains mature content

THE ALL AMERICAN BOYS SERIES

Welcome to Merlot, CA, an idyllic all-American town in wine country where love is in the air, the boys are grown as fine as the wine, and the town is a breeding ground for second-chances, weddings, and brand-new beginnings.

The All American Boy Series gives you a taste of 15 of your favorite bestselling authors' original stories in this shared world experience. All books are standalone but may include cross-over in characters or scenes.

Grab a glass of wine, put your feet up and let us whisk you away to wine country.

The series includes the following books:

Sierra Hill The Boy Next Door
Poppy Parkes Boy Toy
Evan Grace The Boy Scout
Emily Robertson The Boyfriend Hoax
Kaylee Ryan and Lacey Black Boy Trouble
Kimberly Readnour Celebrity Playboy

Marika Ray Backroom Boy
Leslie McAdam Boy on a Train
KL Humphreys Bad Boy
Nicole Richard Hometown Boy
Remy Blake That Boy
Stephanie Browning The Boy She Left Behind
Stephanie Kay About a Boy
Renee Harless Lover Boy
SL Sterling Saviour Boy

Chapter 1

CORD

Pain. It's my first waking thought. Every inch of my body hurts with an indescribable agony. What the hell happened to me? I feel like I've been run over by a train. Twice.

Trying to think is tiresome, like trudging through knee-deep mud. I can't figure out the source of my suffering with my eyes closed, and I'm concerned with what I might find when I open them.

Groaning out my misery and trepidation, I force my eyelids open into tiny slits. The bright light feels like someone has taken a hammer and chisel to my forehead. Gasping, I squeeze my eyes shut.

"Cord, we're right here." I hear my mom's soft, soothing voice, and emotion fills my chest. I push it down; now's not the time for tears. I need answers and my parents can give them to me.

Clenching my teeth, I force my eyes open, blinking repeatedly until the pain in my skull somewhat lessens. Peering down my body, I realize I'm in a hospital bed. I don't notice anything out of the ordinary—no casts on my legs, and I can wiggle my toes.

Rolling my head to the side, I find my mom sitting in a chair. “Mom,” I croak. My throat is beyond dry.

“Here, sweetie. Take a sip.” She brings a straw to my lips and I draw in a mouthful of water. It’s icy and almost too painful to swallow, but it provides instant relief.

“Thank you.” I sound more like myself. Glancing over my mom’s shoulder, I find my dad standing there, silent and resolute as always. A hardworking farmer, he’s a man of few words. He’s a great role model for a son to have. I’m sure he wonders where he went wrong with me. Everything he stands for, I’ve rebelled against.

“Where am I?”

“St. John’s Hospital. You were admitted last night. How are you feeling?” Mom asks, concern wrinkling her brow.

“I feel like shit. How do you think I feel?”

“Son, watch your language,” Dad snaps.

“Hey, Dad. No, don’t worry, I’m fine,” I droll. At least my sense of humor isn’t injured.

“You have no one to blame but yourself. You’re lucky to be alive,” he barks.

“Bill, settle down. Yelling at him isn’t going to help the situation any,” Mom jumps in.

“Carol, nothing ever helps when it comes to him. He won’t be happy until he kills himself or someone else.” My dad’s angry with me, and judging by my current situation, it’s well directed. In my twenty-one years, I haven’t given my folks many reasons to be proud of me, but I can’t remember a time when they both looked so disgusted.

Maybe they’ve finally reached their limit. I knew this day would come sooner or later. In fact, it’s long overdue.

“What happened to me?” I ask.

“You don’t remember?” my mother questions.

"No. It's all a blur and it's too difficult to try to work out through the fog in my brain."

"You went to a party to celebrate being done with finals, got drunk, then you drove home and wrapped your car around a goddamn telephone pole."

Jesus. "Did anyone else get hurt?" My voice shakes. I might not have much regard for my own mortality, but I don't want to hurt anyone else.

"No." Mom places her hand over mine on the blanket. "Thankfully, no one else was involved."

I shutter my eyes, fighting the sting of relieved tears. A knock on the door has them snapping open, and a woman appears. My parents are quick to get out of the way, moving to stand by the windows.

"Hi, I'm Dr. Moody." Stopping at my bedside, she smiles. "Do you remember last night at all?"

"No, but my parents filled me in."

"You sustained a concussion and you're pretty banged up. We couldn't find any signs of broken bones or internal bleeding. Your CAT scan looked good. You're a lucky young man."

"I don't feel lucky," I grumble.

"How's your pain today?"

"Excruciating."

"How does your head feel? Any brain fog or trouble thinking?"

"Yeah. I feel like my brain is wearing a knit cap. It feels heavy. Is that normal?"

"It's a common concussion symptom. You may have sensitivity to light and some dizziness too. How would you like to go home?"

"I can leave?"

She smiles, nodding. "I'm going to discharge you with

instructions you'll need to follow. As long as you promise to take it easy, I'll let you leave. Can you do that?"

"Sure."

"Head injuries aren't a joke. You need to take your recovery seriously. Once you've had a concussion, it's easier to become concussed again. So that means no sports or physical activities for two weeks at the minimum. At that point, you'll need to follow up with your primary care physician."

"Okay."

"And if you're having any complications before then, you should return to the E.R. immediately.

Dr. Moody looks toward my parents. "Do you have any questions for me?"

"No. Tomorrow, I'll make sure he books the appointment with his doctor," my mom informs her, as if I'm still a child.

"Great. She pulls a packet of papers and a pen from the pocket on her white coat. "Here are your instructions." She hands them to my mom and turns back to me. "I need your signature." She hands me the pen and points to the blank line.

My eyes strain to focus as I write my name. I'm sure it's barely legible, but she accepts it just the same.

"If you have any questions, my number is included on the papers I gave you. Good luck and take it easy."

THE RIDE HOME is filled with silence so tense it feels brittle. If one word is uttered, surely it will shatter the air around us into thousands of glass splinters.

Once my dad parks his truck in the driveway, I can't get

out of the extended cab fast enough. I can't remember ever being so happy to be home.

Walking to the front door, my gait is slow and unsteady. I'm not sure if it's an effect of the head injury or because I'm hurting in general.

Crossing the threshold, I wordlessly shoot straight to my room. I know my parents are angry and they want to talk to me. My dad was practically vibrating with pent up anger for the duration of the drive. Obviously, I need to avoid having that conversation at all costs. I realize I fucked up royally and have no plans for a repeat performance.

Sinking onto my bed, I lie down with a groan and toe off my sneakers. They make a dull thud as they hit the floor. One of the nurses gave me a pair of scrubs to wear home and I'm too tired and achy to change out of them.

"We need to talk." I blink a few times and rub my eyes. My dad is standing beside my bed. Gazing at the clock on my nightstand, I realize I've been home for more than an hour. I must've dozed off.

Just great. My dad can't even give me until tomorrow morning to tear into me.

"Bill, can't this wait until he's back on his feet?" Mom asks, rubbing her hands together. I can tell she's worried, and that makes my anxiety shoot through the roof. If my mom is concerned, then I should be too. My parents have a history of being firm but fair with me. Unfortunately, this latest stunt may have changed that. I can feel a whopper of berating just waiting to be delivered by my dad. I guess I should accept my lot and brace myself. There's no avoiding the inevitable. My fingers curl into the comforter, gripping the plaid material.

"Carol, there's no good time for this discussion. He

needs to know what's going on as soon as possible," Dad says calmly.

Tears fill her eyes. *What the fuck?* Now I'm extremely curious and concerned about what's coming.

"If it weren't for your uncle Ted, you'd be facing drunk driving charges."

"How could they prove I was drinking? It's not like I was conscious and took a breathalyzer."

"Think about the bigger picture, son. You were brought to the hospital where they took your blood. Your blood alcohol level is now part of your medical record."

I look down at my arm, noticing the small bandage in the crook of my elbow. "I never gave them permission to take my blood," I shout, panicked.

"Sweetie, you were unconscious when you arrived at the hospital. They didn't need your permission," Mom tries to reassure me.

"You should've been this worried about drinking and driving. Then you wouldn't be in this predicament," Dad says. Throwing this in my face isn't helping anything. All it's doing is making me angry and defensive. Staring at the white ceiling, I draw in a slow breath and tell myself to relax. I'm not sitting in a jail cell, I'm home in my own bed. Things could be so much worse.

"You have two weeks before your mother and I are taking you to your uncle Ted's house. You'll be spending the summer there to work off the debt you owe him."

"How much money is it? I have savings he can have."

"This isn't about a magical number, son. Your uncle put his neck on the line for you. And now you're going to bust your ass doing whatever he asks of you."

"I don't want to stay there all the time. Why can't I go back and forth a few times each week?"

Dad throws his hands up in the air. "How could you possibly do that? It's a four-hour drive. Not to mention you totaled your vehicle."

Oh, yeah. Forgot about that part.

"Isn't there another way?" I ask, trying not to sound emotional. I don't want to spend the next eight weeks at my uncle's. What about all my stuff? What about all my friends? What about my parents? Won't they miss me at all?

---

*Two weeks **later***

My parents keep their goodbyes brief, and before I'm fully ready, I find myself trudging up three wide steps. I pause at the top, scanning my elaborate surroundings. I've been here plenty of times for family functions and holidays, but at this moment, I feel like a stranger, uncertain about what I'm walking into.

Moving along, I smirk at the shrubs that have been made into fancy shapes by a master landscaper—some are extremely phallic looking. They must have to go to school to learn this shit. Everywhere I look, there's greenery. There's even ivy growing over the front entry of the sprawling stucco house. Despite the grandeur of this place, I'm already longing for the homey simplicity of the ranch house I've lived in since I was born.

Standing in front of the large frosted glass door, I pull my shoulders back, determined to face this situation head-on like the man that I am.

I ring the bell and wait, expecting to see my cousin, Leon, answering the door. Instead, my uncle's steely countenance greets me. "Cord. I'd ask how you are, but I can see. You still look like hell." His gaze lingers on the still healing cut above my eyebrow.

"Thanks, Uncle Ted."

"Come in." He steps back, swinging the door wide so I can fit through with my duffel bags hanging from each shoulder.

The door shuts behind me. "Let's head upstairs and I'll show you to your room." Carrying my large bags, Uncle Ted's fast pace is difficult to keep up with. Of course he didn't offer to help me. I'm on my own. I have a feeling that *on my own* could be the theme for the next two months. I've been at college for three years now; being away from my family doesn't bother me. Except this time it's different. This time, the weight of my parents' disappointment weighs heavily on me. I could practically feel their relief when they drove away.

By the time I reach the top of the staircase, I'm huffing and puffing. Uncle Ted directs me down the hallway to the right, opening the third door.

Stepping inside, I'm pleased to find a queen-size bed that looks mighty comfortable. There's also a TV, a large desk, and a tall bureau for my clothes. All the creature comforts and more than I expected, considering the reason I'm here.

"Get unpacked and settled in. Tomorrow, we'll talk and I'll explain what I expect of you." He walks to the doorway and throws a stern look over his shoulder. "Dinner's at six sharp. Don't be late."

I listen for the sound of his footsteps to retreat before closing the door. Sitting on the edge of the bed, I look around once more. So this is home sweet home for now. The sting of tears hits me hard and has me gritting my teeth. I like to think of myself as some hardass who doesn't need anyone. I'm a grown man for fuck's sake. But right now, I feel like a fraud because I'd give just about anything to be back at home and have my mom telling me everything's going to be fine.

Chapter 2

PENELOPE

It's ten thirty in the morning, and the moving truck has just pulled into the drive. I glance around the empty living room, still in disbelief that I've managed to pack up my whole house, and pretty much my whole life, into nothing more than a dozen boxes.

When Eric and I bought this house, I remember being on cloud nine.

Leaving the city, winding down, and getting ready to start our family was everything I had ever wanted. I was high on all the future plans we'd made.

But now, the four walls don't hold the same hope, and any good memories we made have been tainted over and over again.

The knock on the door stops me from thinking about the past and reminiscing about all that was, and all that would never be.

I open the front door and come face-to-face with Nick Flatman, the owner of our local moving company.

"Ma'am," Nick greets.

"For the hundredth time, Nick, call me Penelope. How are you?"

He smiles softly, his features creasing with the change in his expression. "You're the first and the last job of the day. A nice easy run."

"Thank you for doing this."

"Not a problem. Just wish it were under better circumstances."

I smile through the wave of awkwardness his comment brings. The reminder that in Merlot, California, everybody knows everybody's business. Especially mine.

Ending the conversation, and the possibility of talking about the ending of my marriage, I widen the door and shift my body to the side, so my back rests against the wood.

"Please, come inside. Everything is ready for you in the living room." Nick steps over the threshold and I point in the direction of where the boxes are situated. "It's the first entryway to your left."

A few seconds later, his son Kobe jumps down from the truck, tips his head at me in greeting, and heads on inside to assist his dad.

I do my best to stay out of their way and fiddle around on my phone, arranging my calendar and answering emails.

The good thing about owning your own business is you can delegate most tasks and pick and choose when to spend time on your business or your broken marriage without having to explain yourself to anyone.

With a box I assume to be the last one in hand, the father and son team stop in front of me and Nick tips his chin up at me. "Are we still good to head to the other location?"

"Yes," I confirm enthusiastically. "I've got the key, so I'll drive ahead and open it up for you."

Running through a mental checklist, I walk through

every room in the house and make sure nothing's been left behind. When I'm satisfied with the way I've left the place, I lock up quickly, not giving myself time to acknowledge the sudden sense of closure, and climb into my car.

It only takes another fifteen minutes to arrive on the other side of town, where my new house is. The driveway is big enough for both vehicles to park side by side.

I open up the garage door and instruct them to leave everything inside. All the furniture I've ordered will be arriving throughout the week, and I don't really want to unpack any of my belongings until I've set up the house the way I want it. The only thing I need, which is already sitting in my place, in pieces, waiting to be assembled, is my California king bed.

Because nobody wants to sleep on the bed they shared with their ex-husband.

I putz around the house for a little while longer, running through my mental checklist and feeling somewhat satisfied, before leaving for my appointment.

It's another fifteen minutes till I pull up at my lawyer's office, and I'm feeling somewhat accomplished and a little bit apprehensive.

If anyone had told me six months ago that I would feel almost giddy about signing my divorce papers, I would've told them they didn't know me at all.

Because six months ago, I was devastated.

Today, after slowly closing the door on this chapter of my life, not so much.

Heading straight for the office, I'm not surprised to see Janine, the receptionist, waiting for me with her megawatt smile and positive attitude. It's obvious she loves her job, and whether she knows it or not, her warmth has been exactly what I've needed every time I've stepped into this building.

"Good afternoon, Penelope. It's so good to see you again." She gestures to the row of seats lined up across the back wall of the room. "Please make yourself comfortable. Mr. Renner won't be long."

Another five minutes pass and Janine ushers me inside to where Ted Renner, my lawyer, is waiting for me in the meeting room. He sits at the head of the oval-shaped meeting table, and perpendicular to him is an empty chair and a stack of papers waiting to be signed.

"Hey," I greet as I take my seat.

"How are you? Are you ready?"

I pick up the pen and flip over the first page of documents, hoping to extinguish the small talk, not wanting to lose my nerve. "As ready as I'll ever be."

Noticing my eagerness, he points at the sticky tabs poking out of the papers. "You don't have to read everything if you don't want, nothing much has changed since we wrote it up, and Eric didn't contest a single thing. Just sign where the arrows are and you'll be good to go."

Swallowing hard, I start the process, signing my signature over and over, right next to Eric's already scribbled one.

It becomes tedious, and my hand cramps a little, but by the time I reach the last page, I feel the remaining connection to my past finally slip away.

I did it

Exhaling loudly, I drop the pen and let myself relax into the leather chair. Ending my ten-year-long marriage wasn't something I wanted to do, but rather it became the only option I had left. Backed into a corner, it was either fight or flight, and after fighting and failing, I finally chose flight.

I finally chose *me*.

"How does it feel to officially be divorced?" asks Ted, his question instantly bringing me back to the present.

"I didn't think I'd get here," I admit honestly. "Thank you so much for helping me with all of this."

Ted Renner is Merlot's best attorney. And for the last six months, he's turned into somewhat of a confidant as I navigated the uncharted territory of my new life, going above and beyond his duty as my lawyer.

"It was my pleasure." He swivels his chair in my direction, straightens his back, and buttons up his blazer. For a man in his forties, he sure does scrub up nicely. He's a gorgeous silver fox, with kind eyes but a shrewd tongue. It's easy to see why he's the best at what he does; luring opponents in just enough to trust him, only to slice them down till there's nothing left.

Taking a deep breath, he places his hand over mine, something he's never done before. "I was actually hoping we could go out and celebrate."

"Go out and celebrate?" I echo.

"Well." He swallows hard and rubs his free hand over the back of his neck. "Since I'm no longer your lawyer, I was hoping it would be more like a date."

"A date?"

He shakes his head and chuckles awkwardly. "I'm sorry, I'm doing this all wrong," he stammers. "I didn't mean to overstep."

This apologetic, nervous side of him has yet to be seen, and in fact, is quite endearing, but I don't think it's enough to have me agreeing to a date with him.

"Look, Ted." I use his first name, hoping he can hear the sincerity in my voice. I slowly stand up and face him. "You are a wonderful man, but I just don't think I'm there yet. It would seem insensitive of me to agree to something with no clear vision of a future. You deserve better than that."

"I had a feeling you'd say that," he says, his voice full of disappointment. "I was hoping these last few months were kind of proof of how good we could be together."

I'd be lying if I said I didn't know what he meant, because he's right, for the most part we're compatible. But that's just not enough for me right now. I'm carrying so much baggage and so many insecurities when it comes to sex and relationships, that If I'm going to step out of post-divorce hibernation, I don't want to be just compatible. I want us to have something undeniable. Something that is impossible to walk away from. Something that feels like taking a breath of fresh air after what I've been through.

This isn't that.

"But if you change your mind," he continues. "Please, please let me know."

Placing my other hand over his, I slip my fingers through his and give them a little squeeze. "Ted Renner, I am absolutely flattered by your interest, but I'd be doing a disservice to you if I said yes. You deserve better than what I can offer. You deserve more."

Leaning forward, I place a soft kiss on his day-old scruff and pull back.

"Thank–"

"Mr. Renner." A loud voice booms through the intercom, startling me and interrupting my gratitude.

Ted expels a loud sigh, untangles our fingers, and pulls the handset directly in front of him. He presses a button before lowering his head and talking into the built-in speaker. "Yes, Janine, how can I help you?"

She responds immediately. "Your nephew is here to see you."

He raises his finger off the button and groans, almost like he's forgotten I'm still here or that his nephew was arriving today.

"Do you need me to leave?" I ask him quickly.

"No. No. Not at all. You may as well meet him since you'll be seeing him around town soon enough."

"Is his family new to the area?" Knowing that Ted doesn't have any extended family here in Merlot, it's not unusual to know everyone you bump into and to take notice of those who aren't from here. The majority of us are transplants from the city, but we've all now been here long enough to call this place home.

"No, he's here on a mandatory vacation." I raise an eyebrow at his cryptic reply. "He got in trouble with the law, and living here is his punishment."

"Doesn't sound like much of a punishment to me."

"That's because you're not the one completing required community service hours and trying to get into my good books."

"Sir." Janine's voice interrupts us again. "He's asking if he can come in to see you," she continues in a hushed whisper. "He's rather agitated, and I'd rather not have to deal with him."

Ted huffs. "Send him in."

I don't know what I'm expecting when Ted's nephew walks though his office door, but my body's visceral reaction to him isn't it.

The first thing I notice is his build. He's ridiculously tall, his shoulders broad, his arms looking like they've been sculpted out of stone.

He's all muscle and athleticism, but it doesn't stop there. His jawline is sharp, and his eyes are an intoxicating mix of forest green and honey brown.

He's both sexy and beautiful, looking like an underwear model with one too many items of clothing on.

The fact that he's Ted's nephew immediately clues me in to the fact that he's significantly younger than me, therefore, unabashedly ogling him is basically a crime.

But I don't stop. Not even for a second.

He holds all my attention and I can't figure out why.

He stands in the doorway, and Janine scurries along, seemingly happy to be rid of the young man. He looks over his shoulder, smirking at the older lady, almost impressed with how uncomfortable he made her feel.

"Cord," Ted barks. "I thought I told you to wait for me at home?"

Cord turns back around, but instead of looking at his uncle, his eyes land on me. My skin tingles from that one look, and my cheeks heat in absolute embarrassment that a stranger could make me feel such magnetism in less than sixty seconds. If he didn't catch me checking him out before, there's no denying now he knows what I'm thinking about.

"It was boring," he answers, still looking at me. He grazes his bottom lip with his teeth and winks at me. "Plus, I wanted to see what Merlot has to offer."

Chapter 3

CORD

"Cord," Uncle Ted calls out, dragging my gaze from the attractive woman next to him, but not before I notice the way my thorough perusal has her cheeks flushing. He raises one dark eyebrow sardonically. "If you're bored, I'm sure I can remedy that."

I cross my arms over my chest. "I didn't realize I wasn't allowed to leave the house. If that's the case, I might as well be in jail."

"If you equate staying with me to being in jail, you better thank your lucky stars you're not sitting in a cell right now."

"Don't you mean I should be thanking you?" I retort.

"I don't expect your thanks. Your dad has already thanked me, though it wasn't needed. I'd do anything for my brother."

I chuckle. "Obviously. You're stuck with me, after all."

He shakes his head. "I didn't say that, you did." The mystery woman touches his arm. "Ted, I think I should be going."

He smiles down at her with genuine affection. Is this his girlfriend? "Penelope, I'm sorry for my lack of manners. This is my nephew, Cord. Cord, this is Penelope, a client and friend of mine." So he's been friend zoned. I smile. Guess that answers my question.

Stepping forward, I catch a hint of her soft, subtle perfume. Capturing her extended hand, our palms meet, sending a warm tingle of awareness through me. Our eyes connect, green caressing golden brown, and lock on like I'm the missile and she's my target. I lose my breath for a brief moment, reacting like I've been unexpectedly punched in the gut. Dragging in a nostril-pinching breath, I say, "It's nice to meet you."

Her smile is tentative. "Likewise." She turns toward my uncle, breaking our powerful connection, and I breathe easier. "I'm going to head back to my new house and see if I can get my bed frame together. If I start soon, I may be lucky enough to get it done by bedtime."

"It's not assembled already? Why didn't the delivery crew take care of it for you?" Uncle Ted questions.

She raises an elegant shoulder in a half shrug. "There was a mix up when I ordered everything. Apparently, I didn't pay for assembly, and since they had to get to their next delivery appointment, they didn't have time to take care of it for me. I guess that'll teach me to double check things I order online."

He rubs a hand on her upper arm. "It was an innocent mistake, nothing to be ashamed or embarrassed about. I think I have the perfect solution to your problem." His head swivels to me. "Cord will head over to your place with you now and take care of everything. I'll swing by on my way home and pick him up."

"I'm an adult who can make decisions for myself," I snark.

"You lost that ability last week when you totaled your car," Uncle Ted retorts.

I bite down, forcing myself to remain silent. I can't really argue with his point, seeing as it's valid and all.

"No, I'm sure Cord has better things to do than help me," Penelope protests.

There are worse things than spending time with a beautiful woman. "As my uncle explained, I really don't. I'm happy to help you out."

She smiles at me, and my chest tightens. "I appreciate your help and will accept your offer. Shall we go?"

I nod. "Sounds good."

"Penelope, I'll be in touch soon," Uncle Ted tells her.

"Thank you again, Ted. For everything. I couldn't have done this without you." She rises on her toes and presses a kiss on his cheek. "I'll see you later."

"You can count on that," he replies. *Man, he's got it bad, but she's not into him.* If she were, she wouldn't have stared at me with such intensity.

I gesture for her to precede me as we exit the office. The secretary isn't at her desk, so we advance right to the elevator without disruption.

The ride down to the lobby is fraught with tense silence. Add in the hot air, and it's stifling and makes it hard to breathe. I rub a hand across the back of my neck while my eyes zero in on the digital numbers counting down the floors as we descend.

When the doors part, we both bolt free of the metal box and hurry toward the exit. We pause on the sidewalk. "My car is this way." She tips her head toward the right, and we move along the sidewalk. She pulls her keys from her purse and clicks the small remote, unlocking the doors on a sleek BMW.

"Nice car," I say before opening my door. We both slide inside, and she wiggles around on the seat.

"Damn, I love leather seats, but they get so hot."

I laugh. "They do, but I'm partial to them. I have them—had them—in my car," I say, correcting myself with regard to the state of my car.

The engine turns over with a soft purr. I've always been about muscle cars that rumble to life, but this baby is the epitome of luxury. I could get used to riding in style like this.

"So, I noticed you spoke about your vehicle in past tense and Ted made a reference about you totaling your car. What happened? If you don't want to tell me, no worries. I don't want to pry. I'm just curious," she rambles on.

"I don't mind telling you. I went to a party, drank too much, and made the worst decision of my life."

"Oh, jeez. Yeah, but you're okay—physically, I mean," she says.

"Yeah, I was lucky. I got banged up pretty good and I have a concussion, but it could've been so much worse."

"Were there any other cars involved?" she asks.

"Nope. Thankfully, no one else was around."

Her eyes briefly flick to me and then back to the road. "You seem remorseful. Unless I'm reading you wrong. Which is possible. It seems I'm not very good at reading men these days."

"I am. I've regretted making the decision to drive that night every single day since. I play the what if game every night before I fall asleep and I'm sure I always will. *What if I had killed someone? What if I'd died? What if I lived but had life-altering injuries?*" Why am I confiding all of this to her? Maybe it's because I've been deprived of my friends and family since the accident.

"I'm a frequent player of that horrid game myself. I won't

bore you with the details of why, but it's the main reason you're riding in this car with me."

My gaze studies her elegant profile, tracing over the straight line of her nose and gently curved forehead. "Deductive reasoning tells me you recently got divorced," I say.

"Am I that transparent?"

"Not at all. But you thanked my uncle and he's an attorney. You mentioned your new house, which could be a product of a marriage ending. And also you bought new furniture."

"Very astute of you," she says, sounding impressed.

"I want to be a police officer," I explain.

"You're naturally observant, so you'll do well, I'm sure."

"I may have screwed up any chance I had by getting in my accident."

"Are you in college?"

"I'm about to start my senior year at California State University in a couple of months."

"You have your whole life ahead of you. Don't get caught up in one bad decision and let it ruin things for you."

"There's been a lot more than one bad decision on my part. I have a history of making them," I confess. Again, I surprise myself with the level of honesty I'm giving her. There's something about her that makes me comfortable confiding in her. She's easy to talk to as well as easy on the eyes.

"You seem like a good person to me," she reassures me.

"You shouldn't be so quick to think the best of me," I rebound. "I'll only prove you wrong." *And have fun doing it.*

"I guess time will tell if I'm right or not," she replies, turning the car into a freshly paved driveway. The house in front of us is a new construction, split level style. She parks in front of the one-car garage. "Here we are. Home sweet home."

"It's nice. I've always liked this style of home."

She removes the key from the ignition. "It's more than enough space for me." We both open our doors and step onto the driveway.

"You don't have any kids?" I ask.

"No. I didn't want any with my ex—I didn't want them."

Her walk is brisk and I allow her the space she seems to want. Maybe my question was too invasive. Unfortunately, I can't retract the words now. But I'm curious why she answered the way she did.

My gaze glides over her gently curved frame as she unlocks the door. She throws a quick glance over her shoulder to me. "Come on in."

Following her inside, the soles of our shoes tap on the shiny new hardwood floors. The space is bright and open. "This is nice." Without any furniture or rugs, my voice echoes.

"Thank you. It's modest compared to the house I left, but it feels more like home already."

"That's great. That means you'll be happy here," I say, wanting to reassure her but not sure why.

She nods. "I can hope anyway." She holds up her finger. "The bedroom is this way." She springs off again, light on her feet, with me trailing behind. "All that needs to be assembled is the bed frame."

Her bedroom is large and empty aside from a nightstand, a bureau, and the headboard leaning against the wall. I point to the area. "Is this where you want the bed?"

"Yes, please."

After I've organized everything, I set one of the side rails against the mounting hole in the headboard, tightening the screws by hand. This would go much quicker if she had a cordless drill. I repeat the process on the other side and grab the footboard from the other side of the room.

"Do you need help with that?" she asks.

"No, thanks. I'm all set." It's not heavy, just bulky. I fasten the long screws into the mounting holes on both sides, and the outer frame is complete.

After I fasten all the slats between the two sides of the frame, it's time to add the mattress. I glance at Penelope. "Now I can use your help."

"Sure."

"We need to place the mattress on the frame. I'll push it from the back and you can guide the front. Just try to stabilize it and keep it on its side." There's no way she could carry it, so this is our only option.

She does a great job following my instructions and, a few minutes later, her mattress is situated on the frame where it belongs. I hold my hand up and she gives me a high five before jumping onto the bed. Landing on her back, she lets out a long groan. "Oh my God. I'm lying on a cloud." *I want her to be lying on me.*

"It's a mattress, how great can it be?" I ask, dropping down next to her. Lying back, I sigh. "Damn, this does feel like a cloud." I turn to look at Penelope and find her interested gaze already on me. An almost palpable flare of desire pings between us, stretching the wordless moment out a beat or two too long.

The moment she becomes cognizant of our precarious position, it washes over her expression like a filter on a picture, and she utters, "Yeah, it's going to be hard to leave this bed every morning."

My mind flashes an image of us naked and entwined on this mattress. If this was my reality, I'd never want to leave.

The doorbell rings, ruining my fantasy. "I guess my ride's here." Reluctantly, I rise from the bed.

Time to head back to my prison.

Chapter 4

PENELOPE

It's not the first night I've slept alone, but the new house, new bed, and fresh sheets may have contributed to the first uninterrupted sleep I've had in months.

It had felt weird to sleep alone after Eric left, but last night, the ghost of him was nowhere to be found.

In fact, I fell asleep thinking about a man who is far too young for me. It doesn't matter how gorgeous he is, or how helpful he was. It doesn't matter how easy it was to talk to him, or how uneasy I felt watching him walk away.

Groaning loudly into an empty room, I grab the nearest pillow and throw it over my face, dramatically screaming into it.

"Get it together, Penelope," I murmur against the pillow. "Divorce doesn't mean you lose your goddamned mind."

My cell rings, and I extend my arm out of the blankets and blindly feel around the top of my nightstand. Raising the pillow off my face, I squint at the screen and reluctantly answer.

"Hello," I greet, my voice groggy from it's lack of use.

"Rise and shine, Pen Pen."

"Delia, why are you so cheerful in the morning?"

"Well, it's not everyday my best friend gets a divorce."

"Hopefully, it's my first and last."

"So, what are you doing today?" she asks.

"I don't know, I figured I should probably go to the store to check and see how they've been doing without me."

Delia's response is drowned out by the sound of my doorbell echoing throughout my house.

"Shit," I say, startled. "I don't know who that could be, I haven't really told anyone I live here."

"You live in Merlot," Delia scoffs. "Since when do you need to tell anyone anything?"

"True." I climb out of my bed and hastily tug my silk wrap off it's hanger and walk toward the front door. "Look, can I call you back?"

"No way," she says a little too harshly. "You said it yourself that nobody knows you live there. What if it's a psychopath coming to kill you?"

"Geez, someone needs to lay off the true crime podcasts."

"Don't you have your doorbell linked to your phone?" she asks.

"No." I keep her on the line as I pick up the pace and keep talking. "I need to buy a new Ring system, but this old-school doorbell that came with the house will do just fine for now."

Whoever it is presses the doorbell again.

"I'm coming, I'm coming," I call out.

Not bothering to check through the glass side panels that flank the front door, I quickly unlock it and swing it open.

"You scheming little bitch." I drag the phone off my ear and tackle my best friend, grateful to be gifted the surprise of a lifetime. "What are you doing here?"

She doesn't answer right away, holding me just as tightly instead.

"I hated not being here for you these last six months."

My eyes fill with unshed tears. Tears of complete relief and happiness. We pull apart, and Delia frowns at me. "Are you okay?"

I go in for a second hug. "I didn't realize how much I missed you."

While the move to Merlot was very much intentional and something Eric and I wanted, leaving behind our friends and family was the price we paid for this little slice of heaven.

At first, it didn't bother me. Technology was, and still is, in its prime, and besides physical distance, I could see and speak to anyone I wanted at any damn time of the day.

But when things started to get tough, and the cracks in my marriage turned into broken chunks, the distance between me and my family and friends felt enormous.

And then after a while, I just felt downright embarrassed. Embarrassed to be so invested in the move. Embarrassed that we were falling apart. Embarrassed because I was a failure.

So then I went through a stage of avoidance and ignoring everyone who reached out. Especially Delia.

With our mothers being best friends, we were destined to follow the same path, which made the time I've been away from her harder than I would care to admit.

"Now come on, Pen Pen, there will be none of that," she says, hiding her own emotions with fake cheer. "I'm in wine country and I came here to get absolutely wasted."

I laugh. It's soggy from the tears, but it's such an unfamiliar sound. *When was the last time I laughed?*

"Okay," I start as I simultaneously guide her into the

back. "Let's stop at the shop first and make sure it's still standing. You can pick a few outfits, then we'll go to the Moscato Resort & Spa, and finally, we'll spend the rest of the afternoon tasting the best wine Merlot, California has to offer.

"Becca, thank you so much for fitting us in today. I know how hard it is to get a last-minute appointment."

Becca waves her hand in front of her face, her cheeks blushing. "Don't be silly, there's nothing to thank me for. Everybody deserves some R&R with their best friend." She focuses her gaze on Delia. "It's so lovely to meet you."

"Likewise," Delia says politely.

"Why don't you two take a seat and I'll bring you out some champagne while you decide on what treatments you both want to get."

"This place is super fancy," Delia muses, her eyes darting all around the lavish lobby.

"Isn't it? I haven't come in a while."

"That's what she said," Delia interrupts with a smirk.

"You never really did grow out of those jokes did you?"

"Can you blame me? You left the door right open with that one."

A young lady appears out of thin air, holding a tray with two champagne glasses, a strawberry in each.

"Thank you," I say, handing Delia hers, then grabbing mine.

"Plus," Delia nudges me when the server walks away, "you probably haven't come in a while."

"Jesus," I hiss. "Can you be any louder?"

"What? Nobody's listening?"

I do a quick scan of our surroundings and then look her straight in the eye. "If you must know, I've been on a journey of self-discovery. I've been trying to fall back in love with sex and have developed a healthy relationship with my sex toys."

"Yes, but getting off using your vibrator isn't exactly the same thing."

"I don't always need my vibrator," I argue. My cheeks heat up just thinking about Cord and how easy it was to imagine him while indulging in a little bit of self-care last night.

"Penelope Schwartz," Delia scolds. "Are you blushing?"

I turn away from her, not sure if I want to bring up the random crush on my lawyer's nephew quite yet.

"Ladies." Perfectly timed, Becca enters the room, explaining a whole host of regulations and introductions, before she ushers us out into the change rooms. "Now, just get down to your birthday suit, slip into your robe, and your massage therapists will be with you shortly."

When Becca leaves, Delia holds my stare. "Don't think I've forgotten about this," she threatens. "You know I'll get it out of you."

Not generally shy to change in front of one another, I use this opportunity to step into one of the stalls so she can't see my face. "You're making a big deal out of nothing. There's nobody."

"Oh, I know," she says, completely ignoring me. "It's your lawyer, isn't it. You're always smiling when you talk about him and you've been spending *a lot* of time with him."

I'm not surprised she noticed that about Ted. But after seeing Cord and remembering the way my body responded to his presence, I know it was the chemistry that was missing and one of the more obvious reasons I could never entertain the idea of a relationship with Ted.

I step back into the main area, both Delia and I now wrapped in the comfiest and softest material either of us has ever felt.

"So, is it Ted?" she persists.

Holding her gaze, I chew on the inside of my lip in contemplation.

"Pen Pen," she coaxes.

"It's his nephew."

AFTER BLURTING out the most ridiculous confession to ever come out of my mouth, I insisted Delia not ask any questions because there isn't anything to tell. The man was gorgeous. Sexy. Hot. Every possible adjective I could ever come up with still wouldn't be enough to explain the perfect specimen of a man he is.

But by the time we finally sit down for an early dinner at the winery restaurant, it seems Delia can't maintain her silence any longer.

"Well, are you going to do anything about it?"

"Anything about what?" I ask while shoving a mouthful of caesar salad between my lips.

"The nephew."

"Please don't call him that," I chide. "It makes me feel like a criminal."

"He's legal, isn't he?"

"And in college," I add.

"Oh my god," she squeals. "This is perfect for you. You need a summer fling."

"I beg to differ," I murmur.

"Come on, Pen, let loose a little." She holds my stare and places her hand over mine. "What happened between you and Eric? What he did and how it crushed your confidence? I know we can't turn back time and pretend that part of your life never happened. But you sure as hell can make up for it now by living a little and giving yourself some much needed TLC."

"And you think a twenty-one-year-old is how I need to make that happen?"

"I'm just saying I bet he could give you the *perfect* version of tender loving care."

I snort, and we both laugh at my unladylike slip up.

My phone vibrates on the table and Delia swipes it up.

"It's Ted," she supplies. "He said. 'You're welcome. Always happy to help.'" She places the phone down. "What's he talking about?"

"I sent him a text thanking him for all his help and to tell Cord I said thank you for helping with the bed."

She claps excitedly and squeals, confusing me. "What did I miss?"

"This is perfect. Why don't you buy Ted a bottle of wine to say thank you?" She gestures around us. "What says thank you better than wine from Merlot's finest?"

"Wouldn't that be giving Ted the wrong idea?"

"Well, maybe, but if it means you can 'accidentally'"–she hooks her fingers like air quotes–"bump into your summer fling, then why not?"

"He's not my summer fling."

"But he could be."

I try to regulate the butterflies fluttering in the pit of my stomach at Delia's planning and insinuations. Am I really contemplating jumping into bed with my lawyer's nephew?

"This is stupid," I lie while my body tightens at the very

idea of being on top of him. Underneath him. Pretty much any visual of my lips being attached to his as the bare minimum works for me.

"Your cheeks are red again," Delia points out.

"Just drop it."

She doesn't say another word. Instead, she rises and walks away toward the restaurant bar. I watch her as she smiles with Callie, the manager, showing off her teeth and seemingly a lot more comfortable with Merlot life than I expected. Callie pulls out the wine list and points to something written on the decorated chalkboard behind the bar.

Another five minutes of them talking passes and finally Callie goes into the back cellar only to return with three bottles of wine.

Delia sits back down at our table and hands me two out of the three bottles.

"What are these for?" I ask

"These are your thank you gift to Ted and his nephew."

"Delia," I warn.

"What?" she says unapologetically. "I expect a thank you when his twenty-one-year-old dick fucks your brains out."

Chapter 5

CORD

Day number three of my prison sentence has me outside in the backyard. I've been here for most of the day. Uncle Ted left me a list of tasks I "must" take care of. He made sure to let me know he expected each item checked off before he returns home from work. And specifically ordered me "not to do a shoddy job," which made him sound way older than he is. I even looked up the meaning of the word just to make sure I had it right.

Talk about going the extra mile.

My dad has never uttered the word shoddy once in my entire life, and he and Ted are brothers. Which leads me to believe it's a word adopted by my uncle since he seized life by the canines and became filthy rich. And now, he has a talent for making anything he says sound pretentious.

"Hey, whatcha doin'?" My cousin, Leon, walks over.

"What does it look like I'm doing, Einstein? I'm cleaning the patio furniture."

He tsks, but that's normal for him. He turns his nose up at the idea of any sort of labor. "But why?"

"You know why. I'm working off my sentence," I remind him.

"You've been busting your ass for three days already. How much more do you have to do?"

I grimace. "Approximately fifty seven more days."

"That sucks, cuz. Want me to see if I can get my dad to lighten up on you?"

As tempting as his offer is, I can't accept. I did the crime, and now I'm doing the time. As an adult, I'm lucky I'm not locked up doing jail time. Or I could've been put on probation. To show my gratitude, I'll suck up whatever Uncle Ted dishes out. I might not be happy about it, but I'll take care of whatever he asks of me.

I shake my head. "Nah, I can handle this."

"Do you want some help?" he asks.

"You're going to help me?" I smirk. His offer is as empty as the call log on my phone. I haven't heard from my parents once.

"Fine, you got me. I was trying to be nice, but it's too much work."

"Get out of here and do whatever it is you were going to before you came out here."

"I'm heading to a friend's for a party. You want to come?" He looks conflicted about leaving me.

"I'll be at least another hour. You just graduated high school. You don't need to worry about me. Go hang with your friends while you still can."

"Yeah, but you can buy us beer," he says, revealing his motive for inviting me.

"That's not gonna happen. I'm in enough trouble already."

"Don't be a pussy. No one would find out," he replies.

"Leon, don't insult me, because you're not getting your way. I owe your dad a lot, and out of respect for him, I'm not contributing to you and a bunch of other eighteen-year-olds getting drunk."

"You could chaperone the party," he suggests.

"I'd still be in trouble if we got caught."

"Whatever, dude. It's your loss. There will be a ton of hot girls there."

"Thanks for looking out for me, but eighteen is too young for me. My tastes run to women my own age."

And a particular older woman I met yesterday.

"No problem. That's less competition for me." He fist bumps me. "Don't work too hard, cuz."

"Yeah. I'll try not to."

"I'll be home later. Don't wait up." He hurries off without another word.

"See ya," I call out prior to him entering the house and closing the french door.

Taking the spray bottle full of water mixed with dish detergent, I spray the wrought iron chair until it's well saturated. Clutching the small scrubbing brush, I clean every scrolling nook and cranny at the top and wash the remainder of the chair with a wet sponge.

After I've given the entire surface a thorough rinse with the hose, I tug my t-shirt over my head and mop the sweat from my brow. Without a cloud in sight, the sun's powerful rays beam down on me, burning the top of my head and shoulders.

Moving on to the next chairs, I focus on my task and complete the cleaning phase as fast as possible. I still need to wax them all, but they need time to dry first. Stripping off my shorts poolside, I dive into the crystal clear water and swim the length before surfacing. A groan slips from my lips as I push off the balls of my feet and raise my legs until I'm floating on my back.

The water blocks out all sounds around me. The combination of the tepid water beneath me and the radiant sun above me is a perfect combination, and I lose track of time for a bit. What was supposed to be a quick dip in the pool has turned into a time suck I can't afford. I should get back to work before Uncle Ted catches me.

Boosting myself over the side of the pool with only my boxer briefs on, I push my hair from my eyes. Not having the foresight to grab a towel, I stand on the patio letting the water run down my tall frame. The click of the french door closing has me looking up. Penelope stands before me.

"Oh." Her mouth opens and closes in blatant surprise.

I smile. "Hi." I'm happy to see her. She's a welcome surprise and a worthy distraction.

Her gaze lowers to my chest, following the slowly trailing beads of pool water as they continue down my stomach to be stopped by my boxer briefs. The same wet boxer briefs are molded to me, exposing the blood-pumping effect her blatant scrutiny has on my body.

"Hello, Cord." Her voice is breathy, revealing I'm not the only one who was affected by her checking me out.

"What brings you over here?" I'm glad she's standing in front of me, but I'm curious as to why.

She holds up the bottles of wine. "I brought you and your uncle each a thank you gift."

I move closer, angling the bottle of wine toward me so I can read the label. "Looks good to me," I say, like I'm some wine aficionado. When in reality, the only wine I've drunk were a few sips from my mom's glass when I was a teenager. "Would you be interested in sharing it with me?" Her eyes dart up and down my frame, lingering on my groin each time. She licks her lips and her nervousness is obvious. "Uh... uhm..."

"After I get dressed, of course," I cut off her refusal before it happens.

"Uh, sure," she replies.

Bending over, I grab my basketball shorts and pull them on. Smiling at Penelope, I hold out my hand and wrap my fingers around the widest part of the bottle. "Make yourself at home. I'm going to find a corkscrew and some glasses. Be right back." In the glass of the door panes, I see her reflection sinking down on one of the cushioned loungers. Hurrying inside to the kitchen, I grab glasses and a corkscrew and then I pause, wondering if she's hungry. Searching the pantry and fridge, I look for normal snacks but apparently, my uncle doesn't believe in simple things like chips and dip. I end up throwing some grapes, cheese, and crackers on a white dinner plate and hope for the best. Even his snacks are pretentious.

Back on the patio, Penelope is still seated, so I choose the chaise next to hers and set the plate on the small table between them. Getting the cork out is easier than expected, and I pour the red wine into the glasses, ignoring the fact that I'm supposed to be waxing the furniture. With Penelope's arrival, my need to do the right thing has suddenly been put on hold.

Taking the offered glass from me, our fingertips brush, creating a punch of desire that slams into my gut. I suck down a mouthful of wine, wishing it were whiskey, or anything strong enough to dull my senses or numb my body's reaction to her. Yesterday, she looked beautiful, but today, in her casual shorts and shirt, with her long, black hair flowing free around her shoulders, she's flawless. We're sitting facing each other, our knees so close they could easily bump.

Spreading my legs, I lean forward. "This is good." I hold up my glass. "Thank you for the gift."

"I'm glad you like it."

"In the future, if I help you out with anything, you don't need to buy me a present."

She shrugs. "I probably will anyway."

I raise a brow. "But I'm telling you it's not necessary." Her eyes briefly lower to the stone pavers beneath our feet before swinging up to meet mine. "Maybe you just wanted an excuse to see me," I offer, but she doesn't respond. "Yes? No? Maybe?" I prod, on the edge of my seat. "Answer me." My heart feels like it's sprinting inside my chest as I wait for her reply.

Looking conflicted, she presses her front teeth into her bottom lip. She sighs, as if she's reluctant to tell me. "Yes. I wanted to see you. Even though I shouldn't. Even though I'm barely divorced and getting involved with anyone is the last thing I should do."

I take her glass of wine and set it down on the table along with mine. Catching hold of her hands, I skim my thumbs over her smooth skin. "Those are all valid arguments, but I've got one that blows them all away." She looks at me expectantly. "We're adults and we don't have to follow any rules when it comes to spending time with whomever we want."

"True," she agrees.

"So if I'm interested in getting to know you better, there's no reason why I can't—unless you're opposed to spending time with me."

She smiles. "I suppose there are worse ways I could spend my free time."

"All right then. I'm glad we agree." Releasing my hold, I

return her glass of wine to her hand. Picking my own up, I drain the contents in one smooth pull before refilling both glasses. Setting the plate of food on the cushion beside her, I join her on the chaise. Plucking some grapes from the bunch, I pop one between my lips and chew before handing another to Penelope. Taking the fruit without hesitation, she bites off a piece.

The sound of the french door opening has us both turning around. I'm relieved to see it's only Leon. What happened to the party he was going to?

"Hey, cuz," he calls out, sauntering over. Despite the obvious dirty look I'm sending him, he sits on the chaise across from me and I introduce them. We make small talk for a few minutes, but the vibe Penelope and I had going completely shifted with Leon's arrival.

She places her empty glass on the table and rises to her feet. "I should be going. Can you please make sure Ted gets his bottle of wine?"

I nod. "Of course."

"It was nice seeing you again, Leon." She looks at me. "Cord, I'll see you later." She wants to say more but can't with my cousin here.

"Talk soon." I wink and watch her disappear inside the house.

"Nice, cuz," Leon says. "I've always thought she was hot. I know my dad certainly thinks so, but looks like her interest lies with younger men."

"What's that?" I pretend not to understand.

"Nice work. I didn't know you had the game to catch the interest of an older woman."

"You've got an active imagination," I reply.

He looks at me, turning serious. "Cord, your secret's safe with me."

"It's nothing more than some mild flirting and won't

amount to anything, but I'd appreciate it if you kept it to yourself. I'm in enough shit already. No need to add to the pile."

He picks up the bottle of wine, raising it to his lips. "No worries, man," he tells me before he guzzles the remainder down.

"You're in for the night?" I'm worried he might get back in his car. He doesn't need to make the same stupid mistake I did.

"Yeah."

Nodding, I stand and move over to the wrought iron furniture. It's time to get back to work. Unfortunately, these chairs won't wax themselves. Replaying my conversation with Penelope while I rub them down with the car wax makes this task seem a lot less menial.

Chapter 6

PENELOPE

"Your phone is beeping," Shannon, my full-time shop assistant, calls out.

"Who is it?" I walk out of the storeroom, my arms full of dresses that need to be steamed and hung up.

One of the many things that had originally attracted me to the idea of Merlot was the ability to start a new business. With money I'd inherited from my grandmother, it seemed fitting to invest it back into myself. And in Merlot, the competition for a boutique women's clothing store was non-existent. It was perfect.

Sometimes, I wonder if my dedication to my business is one of the reasons Eric and I didn't work out. But then I think of where I would have been these last six months without the ability to completely immerse myself in work when I needed it. To have something that was wholly mine and was untouched and untainted by the divorce. And I've never been more proud.

Extending her arm, she holds out my cell. "It's Ted."

Wordlessly, we do a quick swap, and I swipe at my screen to open Ted's message.

Ted: Thank you for the wine. You shouldn't have.

Not wanting to be rude but feeling really guilty about the whole thing, I tap out a quick and succinct response.

Me: You're welcome.

As soon as I stepped into Ted's house yesterday, I felt like a fraud, an absolute bitch for using Ted for my own personal gain. And when the nerves had dissipated, and Cord and I started to feel comfortable in one another's presence, the moment had ended and I'd spent the whole way home on the phone, abusing Delia for talking me into doing something so insane.

What does it matter if the spark was there? He's twenty-one years old, I'm sure he just about gets giddy at any attention thrown his way.

The quicker I distance myself from Ted and his nephew, the quicker I can just move on to something else. Maybe someone else.

I'd be lying if I said I hated every single one of Delia's ideas, because I don't. Letting off some steam–now that I've signed on the dotted line–is something I could get behind.

I could even maybe download Tinder?

I pick up my phone to download the app, and another message from Ted comes through. I cringe before opening it, a little irritated the shortness of my last text obviously didn't seem to translate well.

Ted: I hope this doesn't seem like I'm overstepping, but I kind of have a favor to ask.

Before I have the chance to reply, another text comes through.

Ted: It's about Cord.

Well, now I'm intrigued.

Me: What is it?

Ted: Paul Gardner and I struck a deal and he's going to

let Cord shadow him and Asher for the next couple of weeks.

Me: And what do you need me for?

The cell phone chimes and vibrates in my hand. "Hello."

"Sorry," Ted says. "I hate texting and figured it would be easier for me to explain this way."

"Okay," I say, feeling slightly weary.

"Basically, I've signed up Cord for a payless job at the police station. It'll be more grunt and gopher work, but hopefully it's enough volunteer hours and servicing a community that the police academy will reconsider his application status and criminal record when the time comes."

"Right, because he wants to be a police officer."

"He told you?" Ted sounds surprised.

"Oh, I did some digging when he helped me the other day," I supply, as nonchalantly as possible. "And while your plan makes sense, what do you need me for?"

"Since the police station is across the road from your store," he answers hesitantly, "I was hoping you could keep an eye on him."

"What do you think he's going to do, Ted? Bail on his hours?" I question, uncharacteristically offended on his behalf. "And wouldn't Paul or Asher tell you first anyway?"

From the conversation Cord and I had, it seems a little out of character that he would. But then, he did get himself into a situation like this in the first place, so maybe Ted has every right to be wary.

"I don't think he will, and I would hope I could avoid any confrontation with the sheriff. But I just want to make sure he's taking this seriously."

"He's twenty-one, Ted. Shit happens, but I think you're underestimating him. I'll be sure to say hello to him if I see him around town, but I honestly don't know what else you think I could do besides offer him a friendly face in a place where he doesn't know anybody."

"Yes," Ted agrees excitedly, and I immediately regret ever opening my mouth.

"That's perfect. Someone he might open up to without the worry that he'll get into trouble."

Considering I was just recently having some inappropriate thoughts about his nephew, being his confidant is not exactly the role in this story I wanted to sign up for.

"Look, Ted," I warn. "I'm barely in the store these days."

"You're right. You've got enough on your plate, I'm sorry," he retreats. "It was stupid of me."

"No," I say, now feeling guilty. "I'll do what I can, but I can't make any promises."

"Thank you, Pen. I really appreciate it."

Ted hangs up and I pull the phone away from my ear, the Tinder app product page still showing on my screen.

Shannon, who must've gone back to the stockroom when I was on the phone, is now beside me, also looking down at my screen.

"Are you downloading Tinder?" she asks.

I think of Cord and how much I want him, then I think of Ted, knowing how much I shouldn't.

"Yes," I answer her hastily. "Yes, I am."

"MORNING, PEN," Chantel, the local barista, greets. "Just the usual?"

"Yes, please." I fumble around for my wallet in my bag, when a sinewy arm stretches over my shoulder and the deep rumble of a man's voice sends shivers down my spine.

"Can you please add a double shot espresso to that order? And keep the change."

Turning to look over my shoulder, I glance up and see Cord looking down at me expectantly.

"Good morning," he says charmingly.

"You didn't have to do that," I protest, feeling a little flustered by his closeness. "I can pay for my own drinks."

"I'm sure you can. But maybe it's my turn to say thank you." His eyes flicker between me and whatever's caught his eye behind me. He licks his lips and lowers his voice. "For the other night."

Chantel returns, moving in slow motion, obviously trying to work out how the new guy and I know one another. And why we're standing so intimately close.

I purposefully step away from him, moving closer to the counter and trying to avoid the rumor mill from gaining any traction. But with a smirk on his face, he just follows, enjoying my discomfort.

"What are you doing here so early?" he asks me.

"I have to open up my store," I supply.

"Is it nearby?"

"Across the road from the police station," I tell him, specifically wondering if he'll divulge the news about his new, unpaid job.

"Oh." He straightens his spine, his whole mood shifting from seductive to interested. "Do you work every day?"

"Who's asking?"

"I'm going to be at the police station every day for the foreseeable future," he explains, not knowing I already know. "Maybe we could do this," he gestures between us, "again sometime."

"And what exactly is this?"

His answer is cut off by a very interested Chantel. "Here

are your drinks," she blurts out. "There's a free table right by the window if you're both wanting to stay for some breakfast."

I drag my gaze away from Cord and raise an eyebrow at Chantel. *Could she be anymore obvious?*

With a knowing smile plastered on her face, she slides the two paper cups across the counter and we simultaneously reach for them.

"Two people enjoying each other's company," Cord continues, like the original conversation had never been interrupted.

While I have definitely thought of ways I would enjoy his company, doing it over a cup of coffee is probably the safest option.

It seems innocent enough, so I agree. "I guess there's nothing wrong with two people sharing conversation over coffee."

The side of his lip turns up into a smirk, and it feels almost like he's mocking me. "What?"

"Nothing," he supplies, shaking his head. "I just find it extremely interesting that you're searching for reasons to justify two adults hanging out together."

"Well, you're just barely an adult," I scoff, and I see Cord's eye flicker in understanding.

"Oh, I get it now. You have an issue with my age."

"I don't have an issue with your age," I lie.

"No, you just have an issue with wanting someone my age."

I swallow hard, wishing my face and my burning cheeks didn't give away all my secrets. My hands begin to get clammy holding on to my chai latte. "Can we not talk about this right here?" I whisper.

He looks around, his gaze slowly taking in his surroundings. "Unless you know somewhere we can go, this is going to have to do."

Unable to take the bystander scrutiny a second longer, I squeeze his forearm with my hand and begin to direct him out of the cafe and we walk the short distance to my store.

He follows dutifully, holding on to my latte as I unlock each lock. When we're both inside, I slam the boutique door with a lot more force than necessary and storm off to the back, needing space. I'm being ridiculous, but I like to have control over the order of things, and his addition to my morning routine, with his chivalrous coffee buying, and his deliberate need to ignore personal space, is just a little too much for me to wrap my head around.

I expect him to be hot on my heels as I walk away from him, to ask me questions, call me out, but what I don't expect when I enter my office is to hear the click of the door closing.

I turn around to ask him what he's doing, but he's already on me. His large hand cups my cheek as his mouth descends on mine with unwavering purpose.

My head wants to argue. My head wants me to tell him to stop. But when his lips land on mine, the voices subside and my usually dormant desire flickers to life, just like it has every time I've been in his presence.

He's more gentle than I expected, one hand sliding around to my neck, the other on my hip, pulling me closer to him. Our bodies are flush against one another, and I can't help but melt into him, my reservations all gone. I slide my hands up his chest, loving the way his hard muscles feel underneath my palms, and he deepens the kiss, his mouth moving against mine softly but urgently. Like he doesn't want to scare me, but he wants me to know he isn't anywhere else but in this moment, with me.

His tongue swipes at the seam of my mouth, and I'm surprised by the small moan it elicits. He tastes like coffee and mint and kisses with a seduction that I feel all the way to my toes.

My body thrums when I feel him press his hard length against me, and my imagination runs wild with all the things we could do behind these closed doors.

My tongue meets his, and I don't even try for dominance. I bask in the taste. In the feel. In the newness.

I revel in the moment, knowing the second we pull apart, everything I'm feeling will be fleeting and reality will settle in. Because this shouldn't be happening. And it definitely can't happen again.

As if he can feel the doubt slipping between us, Cord slows down, the kisses now slow and unhurried pecks.

Eventually, he steps back, and my gaze meets his.

"Cord," I say, my voice shaky, my hands touching my mouth in disbelief. "We can't–"

Wordlessly, he shakes his head, cutting me off.

"We have to talk," I insist.

Again, he shakes his head at me, only this time, he reaches for the door, making his intention *not* to talk very clear. He's past the threshold when he looks over his shoulder and winks at me. "I'll see you later."

Chapter 7

CORD

I don't give her time to argue with me, or to kick me out of the store. Instead, I walk right off, her mouth agape at my audacity.

Once I hit the sidewalk, a grin slowly steals across my face. *Damn. That was some kiss.*

It confirmed everything I'd suspected: our chemistry is off the charts, and she fits perfectly in my arms.

I don't care if she's older than me. Age is an arbitrary factor that's a matter of personal preference. When it comes to Penelope, it's the last thing on my mind. And now that we've kissed, I'm not going to let her use this meaningless difference as a means to keep us apart. Because age is a simple number and nothing more.

Barring a natural disaster that wipes us all from this planet, I plan to make her mine, and that's exactly what I'm going to do.

Judging from the way Penelope kissed me back, curling her body around me, her tongue boldly stroking mine, she feels the same. She just needs to get past the point of worrying about what other people think. I can help her with that. I've been honing that skill for most of my life.

Crossing the street, I progress along the front walkway and step inside the police station. My stomach is a little uneasy. I'm wondering what I'm walking into. Exactly what kind of arrangement did Uncle Ted make? There's only one way to find out, so I step up to the window to check in.

"Can I help you?" the officer asks.

"I'm here to see Lieutenant Gardner."

"Have a seat, and he'll be with you shortly."

Nodding, I turn and walk toward the row of empty chairs along the side wall. *Breathe.* Everything will be okay. What can these guys make me do that's so bad?

EYES WATERING and nostrils burning from the overwhelming scent of bleach, I swirl and scrub the brush around the inside of the toilet bowl. Once I'm done, I flush the bleach and move on to the next one. Altogether, there are four stalls in the men's room and two urinals I've already cleaned. I thought I might throw up when I had to spray and wipe down the urine splatters on the floor and wall. Even with gloves on, it was fucking disgusting. But the worst chore of all was cleaning the outside of the toilets. That involved squatting down and getting up close and personal with a toilet that's had its fair share of hairy asses sitting down on the seat. And cleaning up the smeared fecal matter had me dry heaving a couple times. If I had any food in my stomach, I probably would've lost it. As it stands, I'm still feeling semi nauseous.

Note to self: don't eat breakfast or lunch while working here.

When I'm finally finished, I put all the cleaning supplies back in the appropriate closet and find Lieutenant Gardner in his office.

"Sir, I'm all done with the men's room."

He smiles. "You can call me Paul when you're here."

"Thank you, sir, but it feels too informal. How about Lieutenant?"

"That works too. How was your first day?" he asks.

"Great." I force myself to smile.

He nods. "Good. Tomorrow you can do the women's bathroom."

Fuck my life. "Yes, sir. If you're all done with me, I'm going to get going."

"It's five o'clock. You could've left an hour ago."

Now he tells me.

"Have a good night, sir. I mean, Lieutenant."

"See you tomorrow, Renner."

Once I'm outside, I drag a few long, slow, deep breaths in through my nose, expelling slowly to clear my sinuses and lungs of the bleach fumes. I think the fresh air only makes the chemical smell more noticeable.

Pausing on the sidewalk, I realize I don't have a way home. I can call an Uber or I can walk. While both options have merit, I've been stuck inside the police station all day and could use the fresh air.

Setting off for the start of my four-mile trek, I glance across the street to Runway. Her car is parked right out front. For a moment, I'm tempted to reroute my plans for a chance to see her for a few minutes. However, it'll take me at least an hour or more to get back to my uncle's house as it is.

About a mile into my walk, a BMW beeps and pulls over in front of me. I grin when I realize it's Penelope. Walking up on the passenger side, I peer inside the open window. "Hey there."

"Hey. What are you doing walking out here?" she asks.

"I'm on my way home."

"You don't have a ride?" She seems surprised.

"I don't have a car right now, and my uncle didn't offer to bring me home."

She smiles. "Hop in. I'll give you a lift."

Hell yeah. This definitely makes up for cleaning toilets.

I slip inside her car and fasten my seatbelt. "Thanks. I appreciate this. I'm so hungry, I'm weak."

"Didn't you eat anything?"

"Nope. Just the coffee this morning. I didn't want to make a bad impression on my first day," I explain.

"So you skipped lunch?" she asks incredulously.

"Yeah, it sounds kind of ridiculous, but at the time, it seemed like the best choice."

"Every employee is entitled to a lunch break. Don't skip it again."

"Believe me, I won't. Between the bleach I was cleaning with and lack of food, I was light headed."

She snickers.

"What?" I ask.

"I thought I smelled bleach."

I groan. "I think the scent is burned into my nasal passages forever."

"You just need to replace it with another strong scent."

"I don't have any weed with me," I joke.

"I think I can do even better than weed," she replies confidently.

"That's a tall order. My expectations just shot sky-high." She signals to turn down a street I'm unfamiliar with. "Where are you taking me?" I ask.

"Only to the best pizza place within fifty miles."

My stomach growls loud enough for her to hear, and we laugh. "You won't hear any arguments from me or my stomach."

Five minutes later, we're ensconced in a booth in the back of the Italian restaurant, sharing a pitcher of beer. Swallowing the cold liquid, I sigh with pleasure and set my glass down. "This place smells fantastic, and you were right, I can't smell the bleach anymore. You're a genius." Reaching across the table, I take hold of her hand. Her eyes sweep down to our joined hands as if she's checking to make sure we're really connected. When they creep back up to meet mine it's all I can do not to drag her across the table between us and kiss her—kiss her until every reservation she has about us dissipates. My hand tightens on hers as I prepare to make the kiss an actuality.

"Here you go." The waitress appears holding the large pizza pan. Setting it on the table along with extra napkins, she hurries off.

Goddammit. I can't help but be disappointed at the missed opportunity. Any chance I have to connect our lips, I should be taking advantage of. But at the same time, the steaming, mouthwatering pizza isn't the worst trade-off.

Releasing her hand, I pick up a plate, adding a slice of pepperoni before setting it down in front of her.

"Thank you. I know how difficult it must be for you to remember your manners right now when you're starving." Her eyes tease as well as her words.

Using the spatula, I set a slice on my plate. It barely makes contact with the white surface before my fingers raise it to my mouth. I'm already moaning before I even take a bite because the piping hot slice is giving off the most incredible aroma.

Once my teeth sink into the cheesey mess, I close my eyes and, for the second time today, wish I could freeze time. The first one being Penelope's and my kiss.

"I'm jealous you're having this for the first time," Penelope says, and my eyes snap open. She giggles. “Sorry. I didn’t mean to interrupt your private pizza moment.”

I chuckle. “No apology necessary. Thank you for bringing me here. This is fucking phenomenal.”

“Right? I grab food from here at least once a week.”

We continue to devour the pizza. Okay, I devour most of the pizza while Penelope watches with mild amusement after she’s had her two slices.

I finally slow down on the last slice. “You have single-handedly salvaged my summer.”

“They deliver too,” she tells me.

“I wasn’t speaking about the pizza, Penelope.” I take another bite and hum while I chew and swallow. “Okay, I wasn’t only talking about the pizza.” I wink.

“What are you referring to then?” She pops up a dark eyebrow.

“I meant *you* alone. I can list the ways if that’ll help you understand.

Spending time with you.

Kissing you.

Looking at you.

Talking with you.

Listening to you.

Making you smile.

Do I need to continue?”

She lowers her chin and rubs her lips together. It’s not meant to be flirtatious. It’s her natural reaction, and it makes me wonder if she’s not used to receiving compliments. “I don’t know what to say to all that,” she says, confirming my suspicions. “Thank you?” It leaves her bow shaped mouth as a question.

“You don’t need to thank me for merely pointing out the ways you’ve improved my summer.”

"Actually, I think I do. No one's really said anything that sweet to me before."

"What about your ex-husband?" I blurt out the question before I can stop myself. How could he not compliment her?

"No." She shakes her head. "Not in a long time, and we met in high school. I can barely remember a time we weren't together."

"Until now," I add.

"Until we split six months ago," she corrects.

"Why did you guys divorce? Aside from the fact that he sounds like he didn't appreciate what he had at home." She gnaws on her bottom lip, lost in her thoughts. "Well?" I prod.

Her eyes plead with me not to push for more. "I don't want to tell you."

I force myself to ask, "Why not?"

"It's embarrassing for me."

Catching hold of her hand, I give a gentle squeeze of encouragement and aim my most earnest stare at her. "You can tell me, Penelope. I'm the last person who's going to judge you for something in your past."

Drawing in a deep breath, she shifts on the vinyl seat, sitting a little taller. "My ex was addicted to pornography." I'm so stunned I don't reply, and she continues, "He watched it every waking moment he could."

"Wow. What a dumbass," I say.

"He couldn't help it," she says defensively.

I shake my head, annoyed she's defending him. "That's bullshit. He had *you* at home and he turned to his laptop instead? He's not just a dumbass, he's the king of dumbasses," I announce.

She smiles. "I've been told by a counselor it's like any

other addiction and needs to be treated as such. He got addicted as a young teenager."

"Yeah, he and every other teenage male watches porn. I watched my fair share too. But it's not a replacement for the real deal. Did you guys..." I stop myself from asking.

"Did we have sex?" she asks, and I nod. "We had a normal sex life, or at least what I perceived to be normal, until a couple of years ago. It was like one day a switch flipped and he never wanted sex again. I thought he was having an affair. In fact, I was convinced he was, because what twenty-something guy doesn't want to have sex at all?"

"But it wasn't an affair," I reply, my thumb caressing the back of her hand.

"Nope. It took me a while to figure out how much his addiction was taking over, but when he got busted at work for watching porn, that sure opened my eyes. He got demoted as a result and still, he refused to go to counseling with me. So I went by myself and worked through what I could. Eventually, I got tired of being the only one trying, so I hired an attorney and served him with divorce papers. It probably sounds cold-hearted to just be done with someone after all those years."

"No, it doesn't. A relationship won't last when only one person is invested in making it work."

She smiles. "How did you get so wise at such a young age?"

"I keep telling you age means nothing. Maybe now you'll see the merit in my words."

"I'm seeing a lot of things from a new perspective lately," she admits.

"Does that have anything to do with a certain handsome, intelligent, younger man who's ready, willing, and able to show you how special you are?"

"Maybe."

The waitress swings by to take the empty pan and plates and leave the bill.

Releasing her hand, I grab some money from my pocket and close it inside the small leather folder.

Penelope starts rummaging in her purse. "Let me give you some money."

"It's all set. Come on." I hold my hand out to her. She clasps hold, allowing me to pull her to her feet. She opens her mouth to speak, and I close my lips over hers, swallowing her argument along with her gasp of surprise. This kiss is hardly more than a brief taste, a quick reminder of our powerful chemistry. Drawing back with a smile on my lips, I watch her eyelids flutter open like she's still affected. She smiles back at me before her gaze sweeps around the interior of the restaurant.

"Stop worrying, Penelope. Everyone's too busy eating to pay attention to us."

The ride to my uncle's is spent in silence and over too soon. "Pull over here," I direct, pointing to the side of the road just before the long driveway we need to turn into. "I wish I didn't need to get back here right now." Uncle Ted made it clear he wanted me home by eight o'clock so we could touch base on how my day went. But I'm pretty sure he's already spoken to his friend Paul to see how it went. And if he didn't, it's only a matter of time.

"It's probably for the best." She ducks her chin and my finger is immediately there to raise it back up. "You'll get used to the inevitability of us sooner or later." I wag my finger between us. "This is happening." Leaning forward, I feather my lips across hers, gently coaxing and proving the power behind my bold statement. Whatever has us in its grip is bigger than both of us. The only option is to give in to these emotions that spiral and grow like a vortex every time our lips connect. Burying my fingers in her hair, I stroke my tongue along the inside edge of her soft and pillowy bottom lip. I could occupy myself doing nothing more than this for hours at a time.

Penelope clutches my shoulders, tugging me as close as we can get with the console between us. Her tongue dances with mine, making my head spin and heart take off like a rocket launching behind my ribs.

We're both breathless when we part. I caress her cheek tenderly, and for a few seconds, the world comes to a screeching halt. Nothing else matters. With our eyes locked and our breaths slowing and syncing, we could be the only two people in the world.

Until my phone beeps, shattering our private bubble. Tugging it from my pocket, I see a text message from my uncle.

Ted: Where are you?

I grimace at the ill timed reminder and curse myself for putting myself in such a position that I have to answer to him.

Then again, if I hadn't fucked up, I'd never have met Penelope. Sometimes the best things can evolve from the worst circumstances.

Chapter 8

PENELOPE

It's been a whole week of nothing but foreplay. And when I say foreplay, I mean, we meet at the coffee shop in the morning, kiss in my office before he leaves, and spend the night driving to the next town over to eat dinner, make out, and talk before I drive him home for his eight p.m. curfew.

I need more. I want more.

But I wish I didn't have to be reminded every time I dropped him off in his uncle's driveway that he's a twenty-one-year-old man who has a whole life ahead of him. A whole lot of mistakes to make and a whole lot of sins to atone for.

And I don't want to be one of them.

But I do want to be something to him.

According to Delia, this is supposed to be a summer fling. But according to my head and my heart, this is starting to feel a lot like a relationship. It's got depth, it's got potential. In a short time, it's gotten to be a whole lot more than the last few years of my marriage were, and that scares the absolute shit out of me.

Cord is intense, in ways that I didn't know I liked. He

says what's on his mind. He says how he feels and tells me all the things he wants and doesn't. He's unapologetically honest, and I find it both refreshing and scary. Because while he is that way about everything in his life, he's especially that way about me.

He's breaking walls down, one by one, surprising me at every turn with how much he wants me and how hard he's willing to work for it. And if I'm honest, I don't want him to stop.

Work has been slow today, and after Chantel and I finished changing up the storefront for the week, I sent her home. The bell above the front door of my shop rings and I stop what I'm doing on the computer to look and see who it is.

I'm surprised to see Cord walking toward me with the biggest smile on his face. It makes him look both carefree and careless, a reminder of how he's effortlessly two sides of the same coin.

"I don't know if I should be happy or worried you're smiling so big," I tell him.

Wordlessly, he grabs my hand and leads me to the office. "What are you doing? How come you're here in the middle of the day? I can't just leave the store unattended."

He puts a finger up to indicate I need to give him one second and then he disappears. When he returns, I expect him to provide me with some sort of explanation, but he doesn't say a single thing. Instead, he takes my hand and we walk toward my desk. He takes a seat on my office chair and then tugs me to him.

"Sit," he commands.

I'm wearing a short, floral print, baby doll dress with ruffled hems, so there's little to no discomfort as I maneuver myself atop him.

His eyes never leave mine as his hands slowly glide up my thighs, and my skin pebbles with goose bumps. They stop moving when he reaches the edge of my panties, and I ache in anticipation.

"What are you doing?" I whisper, still holding his stare.

I feel him harden beneath me, and it takes everything in me not to grind myself against him. He brings his mouth to mine, his tongue and lips answering my question.

It feels so different to indulge in him, to want physical intimacy, to actually crave sex. But with Cord, even with the slow pace we've been keeping, my insecurities no longer exist. I'm no longer the woman who's worried about pleasing her man. I'm no longer comparing myself to unrealistic standards or keeping quiet to not 'rock the boat'.

With Cord, we're on an even playing field. It makes me feel sexy, wanted, and extremely satisfied.

The kiss is deep and unhurried, but it turns me on like nothing else. The way he always takes his time, the patience he's displayed, the sincerity he's constantly offering when we talk about my past.

He's a grown, mature man in all the ways that matter me. Age is no longer something that does. I believe that now.

His hands continue to remain still, but he teasingly begins to caress his thumbs up and down my covered pussy. My lips are still on his, but I stop kissing him the second his thumb brushes over my clit.

He smiles against my mouth. "Distracted?" he teases, his fingers still taunting me.

"This midday romp is just a little unexpected, is all," I say breathlessly.

"Do you want me to stop?" He pushes past the fabric and slides his thumb up and down my wet center, deliberately avoiding exactly where I want him.

"More," I murmur before resuming our kiss.

He delivers, but it isn't without a little torture. And when he stops touching me and slips his thumb between our mouths, so we're both licking the taste of me, I'm struggling to find my balance on the edge of this proverbial cliff.

Dropping his hand, he fastens his lips to mine before moving across my jaw and down my neck. In one swift move, he's spun the chair so we're directly in front of the desk and he lifts me up on it.

I fall back onto my elbows, anticipating his next move. His hands push my dress up, exposing my legs and stomach. With a smirk, he hooks his fingers into my panties and drags them down my legs.

My breath quickens as any hint of embarrassment I may have felt falls away, just like my underwear. I'm practically naked, his eyes are burning with desire, and I've never felt sexier.

"I don't know when or how," he growls. "But I need inside of you."

"Do it now," I breathe, needing it just as much.

"No." He circles my clit with his thumb, his eyes focused on the movements. "I don't want to have to rush off after our first time together."

A wave of panic washes over me as I think of these quick stolen moments we've shared, wondering if this is all we're destined to be.

"What if this is all we have," I gasp as he hooks my thighs over his shoulders and slips his long finger inside of me.

"Trust me."

He buries his head between my legs, silencing my worries, and feverishly sucks and licks my clit. He eases two fingers inside of me, and my body effortlessly welcomes them. His tongue and fingers perform a beautifully choreographed dance on my pussy, and every part of me wants to erupt in applause.

It's too much and not enough.

I slide a hand over his head and push him closer to me, wanting as much of him as I can take. His fingers mercilessly pump inside of me, the tips grazing my G-spot at the perfect angle.

"Fuck. Cord. Right. There." Moaning, I arch my back into the air as continuous waves of pleasure ricochet through me. I press my thighs together, locking his head between my legs as his tongue greedily laps at my center.

Slowly, my muscles loosen and my body is nothing more than a sated heap of desires and emotions.

Cord raises his head, his lips shining with my arousal. "You sound like you enjoyed that."

I can't help but laugh at his observation. "I guess you can say that." I reach for him and he rises off the seat and hovers over me.

"Thank you," I say shyly.

He lowers his face to mine. "You don't have to thank me for giving you an orgasm."

"What if I'm just thanking you for being you?"

His expression softens, the desire and lust that is often so visible on his face turning into something more meaningful. Something more permanent.

"I'm on extended lunch break," he says casually.

"Ohh." I drag the word out in understanding. "That explains the surprise visit."

"Was it a good one?"

"The best." I slide my hand down his chest and cup him through his pants. "Want me to return the favor?"

A loud banging on the store door interrupts our fun and

I pull my hand back in a moment of complete shock. "Fuck, that scared the shit out of me."

I push at Cord's chest and he reluctantly stands up straight. "Can't we just pretend you're not here?"

"No." I jump off the desk and run my hands over my dress, trying to rid it of the creases. "But we are going to pretend you're not. Can you stay in here till I see what's going on? Is your lunch break nearly over?"

He looks up at the clock mounted on my wall. "I have another half an hour till I have to be back."

I give him a quick nod and rush out of the room.

My heart beats frantically when I see Ted on the other side of the glass. I try to school my face and nonchalantly open the door.

"Ted, hey," I greet.

"Hey," he says a little out of breath. "Have you seen Cord?"

"Shouldn't he be at the police station?"

"Paul said he gave him an extended lunch break, and Chantel from the coffee shop said I would find him in here."

"Oh." I nervously tuck my hair behind my ear. "I can't say I've seen him. But if I do, is there anything you need me to tell him?"

"I was downtown for a meeting and thought I would tell him myself, but I can just text him. No big deal."

"Okay." I offer him a strained smile while awkwardly holding on to the door. "Is there anything else I can help you with?"

Ted looks surprised at my brush off, but if I thought it would make him leave quicker, I was wrong. "Actually," he says. "Do you want to have some lunch with me?"

We're friends. We've always been friends. Before Cord, saying yes wouldn't have been an issue. But now lunch with his uncle feels wrong and complicated. Not to mention that Cord is currently hiding in my office.

"I'm sorry," I say, shaking my head. "I'm on my own today and I've got so much to do."

"Sure." He rubs the back of his neck. "Maybe another time then."

I nod quickly, and he eventually, albeit reluctantly, walks away. Relieved, I head back to Cord, who's now pacing the length of the room.

"Are you okay?" I ask.

"Was that my uncle?"

"Yeah."

"What did he want?"

"You?"

"Will it bother you if he found out about us?" The question surprises me, and the inability to answer it, even more. "If he found out, would you end it or would you tell him to mind his business?"

I shrug. "I honestly don't know, Cord. I can hardly tell him to mind his business, you're his nephew."

"So that would be the end of it, then?"

Needing to steer away from all the hard questions, I seductively walk over to him and place my hands on his chest.

"You're twenty-one, you're going back home in six weeks and then you'll be back at college. This is ending either way, so we should only be focusing on how much 'fun' we can fit in between now and then."

His face falls momentarily, and the guilt I feel for both lying to him and hurting him makes this much more difficult than I anticipated.

I look at the clock, then back at him. "You've still got fifteen minutes till you have to go back." I reach for his pants and rub my hand over his dick. “How about we pick up where we left off?”

He gives me a half-hearted smile, and it’s enough for me for now. I can work with it and hopefully bring us back to the mood we were both in right before we got interrupted.

“It’s only fair since you’ve already had your lunch.” When I feel his length harden underneath my touch, I keep my eyes on his and drop to my knees. Unbuttoning his jeans, I pull the zipper down and pull his cock out of his boxers. “I can now have mine.”

Chapter 9

CORD

Uncle Ted has expensive taste in all areas, and though I often find this quality pretentious, I must applaud his taste in vehicles. Riding in his brand new Corvette Stingray convertible feels incredibly freeing. It could only be better if I were the one driving. The wind blowing through my hair and the early morning sun shining down on me is the perfect combination.

"What's the horsepower on this baby?" I ask.

He grins. "Four hundred ninety-five."

"Daaaamn. When do I get to give it a test drive?"

His eyes bounce to me and back to the road. "Since your license is currently suspended, that's not going to happen."

"Come on. You can take me someplace deserted where no one will see me driving."

"Hell no, Cord. I'm an attorney. I can't break the law because you want to try out my new toy. You'll have to wait until your license is reinstated."

"Then I can drive this?" I ask.

He nods. "Absolutely. But only if you keep behaving. Which leads me to something I need to talk to you about."

Oh great. "What's up?" I just want to know what's going on.

"I'm heading out of town tonight and will be gone through the weekend. I'll return Monday evening."

"Party time," I joke.

"Yeah, yeah. There'll be no parties while I'm gone. While I'm not naive enough to assume you'll be home early every night, I'm counting on you to make solid decisions. Promise me there will be no trouble while I'm gone." His eyes flick to me, and the weight of that brief glance is heavy.

"I promise I won't get into trouble," I reply, and I mean it. Already, my brain is spinning like a tornado coming up with ideas of how Penelope and I can spend the time together.

"You've been doing well and you need to keep it up. I don't want any phone calls from Lieutenant Gardner telling me you've been arrested."

"You won't get any calls about me. I'll be on my best behavior." My best behavior better involve being naked with Penelope for three days straight. We haven't had any alone time together in a week. And now, Uncle Ted just presented us with the perfect opportunity to delve deeper into the relationship pool. I fully plan on capitalizing on his trip, because who the fuck knows when we'll get another opportunity to spend so much time together. And more importantly, alone time.

Uncle Ted pulls up along the curb in front of the police station and turns to look at me. "If you need me while I'm gone, don't hesitate to reach out." I appreciate how he wants to be there for me if I need him. It makes me a little emotional, and I have to quickly shove the feelings back down before he can tell. He's been more of a father to me lately than my own dad has. I've barely spoken to my dad, and when I have, I can feel his disappointment from four hours away. It weighs heavily on me. What son wants to disappoint his parents?

"I'll be fine. You have my word." I hold my hand out and we shake on it. "Have fun," I tell him.

"It's a work thing, so I'm not counting on much fun. A bunch of stuffy lawyers jammed into a conference room."

"Don't forget egotistical." I smirk.

"Okay, smart ass, get out of my car. I'm sure you have an exciting day of toilet cleaning ahead of you," he says.

I point at him before stepping out of the car. "I knew you were checking in with the lieutenant." I close the door and wave. "Safe travels."

Grinning like a little boy playing with a new toy, he revs the engine, pops the clutch, and steps on the gas, burning rubber just like I would do if I was in his shoes. Of course, I don't know if I'd be doing this if I owned a brand new eighty-thousand-dollar car. He pulls away from the curb with a triumphant shout and a fist pump.

I stand there with a smile on my face, watching until he's out of sight. Seeing this other side of my uncle has been eye-opening. He may be about doing the right thing all the time, but he still likes to have fun. I can learn a lot from him.

I've always struggled with the "having fun while doing the right thing" part. But the weeks I've spent here have already shown me how capable I am of making solid choices. I'm proud of myself for how hard I've been working.

Speaking of work, it's time to get inside and see what Lieutenant Gardner has in store for me.

As far as the days I've spent at the police station go, today hasn't been so bad. I've had a fairly light duty day which has consisted of sweeping all the floors and dusting shelves. My last task has been wiping down everything in the break room, which should really be called the broken room because it seems to be the place all the broken furniture ends up. And yet they still continue to use it.

The large rectangular table wobbles, and the spindles on the back of the chairs have too many cracks to count. The refrigerator hums louder than my grandmother and it's that horrible gold color that was once popular. It's probably at least twice as old as I am.

Cleaning inside of the microwave is like a science lab experiment. I don't think it's ever been tackled before. I'm not sure what is stuck to the sides, but it's taken a lot of scrubbing to get it to chip away.

After I say goodbye to Lieutenant Gardner, I walk outside and immediately look for Penelope's car across the street. We agreed I would meet her at her house once I got out of work, and she offered to take care of preparing dinner. I didn't want her to give me a ride because I need to hit a couple of stores before I go over. Looks like she's already left. Smiling, I think about having her in my arms soon.

Glancing at the time on my phone, I order an Uber to pick me up in another twenty minutes. That gives me just enough time to run in the grocery store and grab what I need.

Unfamiliar with this store, I race through the aisles searching for everything on my list. I pick out two bottles of wine from a local vineyard and two mixed bouquets, because she deserves unexpected flowers from her man. And yes, I am her man, even if she may not be sure. I also throw ice cream and whipped cream in the cart before wheeling it over to the self checkout.

Everything fits in two paper bags, and my Uber is waiting in front when I exit the store. I spend the ride to Penelope's filled with anticipation. I can't wait to see her. I can't wait to kiss her and hold her in my arms.

"Thank you," I shout as I jump from the back seat, collecting my bags. I bump the door closed with my hip and speed walk to the front door. With my arms full, I use the toe of my sneaker to knock the bottom of the door twice.

Penelope greets me with a chest-weakening, beaming smile, and I'm struck with tunnel vision—I forget about everything but her.

"Get in here," she orders, reaching over the bags to pull me along by the neck of my t-shirt. Kicking the door shut, I continue on, Penelope walking backward, still leading me. When we reach the kitchen, she releases my shirt. Setting the two bags down on the small table, I spin around and capture her lips with mine. We share a moan when our tongues meet, and the kiss turns wild. Our teeth clash as we fight to get impossibly closer to one another.

Hands clenching my shoulders, her nails sink into my skin through my shirt. Cupping her chin with one hand and the nape of her neck with the other, I hold her captive as I devour her mouth.

I suck and bite her plump lips and stroke my tongue around hers until our hips buck and grind with unrestrained desire.

"Please," she whispers against my mouth. "Need you."

There's no denying her what she wants—me. And I want her just as much. My fingers find the zipper on the back of her black, sleeveless dress, dragging it down with the smooth buzz of metal on metal. I swear that sound makes my cock even harder.

Tucking my thumbs under the material on her shoulders, I glide the dress down her arms until it falls to her waist. My gaze zeros in on her ample tits and I dive face-first between them as if this is the first pair I've ever seen. They may not be the first, but they're definitely the best.

My nose and lips nuzzle along the deep V while my fingers work behind her back, plucking the small hook free from the loop.

Yanking the lacy garment from her arms, I drop it to the floor, my eyes never leaving her nipples. They're reaching for me, taunting me, begging for my mouth.

Cupping her breast in my hand, I close my lips around one taut peak, licking and sucking while I cup the other in my free hand. I pinch and pluck the hard bud before the pad of my thumb circles and whisks over the tip. "Christ. Your tits are amazing." I bite and suck the top of her breast until I leave a mark. Raising my head, I stare down at it with a smile.

Spinning her around, I place a hand in the middle of her back, guiding her over to the marble countertop. I ease her dress down over her hips and legs and help her step free of the material. A hoarse groan slips free when I see her tiny panties that expose a good portion of each cheek. I seize each side, stealthily working her panties down her legs, over her red stilettos, and onto the floor. "Hold on, baby," I tell her, kicking her feet apart. Dropping to my knees, I pull her hips back. She arches her back like a goddamn fantasy come to life. Slapping her ass, I watch the jiggle before I bury my tongue between her slick lips. I take a long, slow lick all the way up to her clit.

Her palms slap down onto the cold stone surface, bracing her torso while her legs quiver beneath my hands.

Consumed by an unquenchable hunger, I continue devouring every inch of her pussy. A few final swipes of my tongue have her shattering. Her arms give out and she falls to her elbows while I lick up the fruits of my labor of love.

Jumping to my feet, I tear my t-shirt over my head and throw it aside. My jeans, boxer briefs, socks, and shoes are gone in a flash. My hands grip her hips, holding her steady while I guide the tip of my cock to her entrance. "Fuck, I forgot a condom." I back up a step to reach for my pants.

"No. Don't make me wait any longer."

I press the head to her entrance once more. "Are you sure?"

"Fuck me," she cries. Thrusting my hips, I bury myself to the hilt and hold still for a few seconds. My hoarse breaths punctuate the silence as I savor her warm pussy wrapped around my bare cock.

"Cord." She moans my name, and I start to move slowly, watching my cock disappear inside her. Jesus. She's the sexiest thing I've ever seen. I never want this to end, but I've been holding off my orgasm since the moment I tasted her again. I've spent the past week jerking off to the memories of going down on her in her office and the best blowjob of my life. No matter how many times I fisted my cock, it never satisfied my need for her.

Fingertips sinking deeper into her skin, I pick up the pace, pulling her back onto my cock with every forward stroke. The sound of skin slapping drives me on and I slam into her faster and faster. My smooth rhythm turns jerky as my release crashes into me with the power of a tsunami and seems never ending. Knowing my come is jetting inside her has me feeling perverse pleasure. I also feel possessive of her. This is so much more than sex to me, and I want that to be the case for Penelope too. Her pussy is now mine. But I won't be satisfied until I own her heart too.

Bracing my hands on either side of hers on the marble, I

lean my chest on her back and my cock slips from her. I can barely catch my breath. I end up gasping and choking out my words. "You're incredible." Wrapping an arm around her waist, I press a kiss to the side of her neck. Straightening up, I turn her around and fold her into my embrace.

She shakes her head. "I don't know what to say. I've never had sex that was so amazing."

"Me either."

"I've never had kitchen sex before," she confesses, surprising me.

"Another first for me too. I wanted you to have the comfort of a bed, but I couldn't wait any longer."

"You couldn't even take my heels off." She giggles.

"No, that was on purpose. They look sexy as fuck on you and put you at the perfect height for what I had in mind." I smirk.

"I like a man who plans ahead." She tightens her arms around me. Placing my forehead against hers, I close my eyes and focus on how amazing this moment is. How comfortable we are with each other. How right everything about us has felt to me from day one. I'm crazy about Penelope and she's crazy about me. However, getting her to admit those feelings is a whole 'nother matter, and I'm running out of time before I have to head off to school.

"I didn't get a chance to tell you that my uncle is out of town until Monday evening."

She opens her eyes wide. "Does that mean you can spend the time here with me?"

"Yep. That's exactly what it means." I grin.

She squeals and pulls my head down for a quick kiss. "This is the best news ever. We don't have to sneak around. You can sleep over. We can cook together. We can watch TV together." With every item she lists, her eyes sparkle more.

"We can do all of those things and more," I say. "How about we start with some nourishment." I rub my stomach. "I need sustenance if I'm going to be ready for rounds two and three."

"Two and three?" She looks surprised.

I nod. "That's what I said." I tap the tip of her nose with my fingertip. "Just consider it one of the many perks of dating a younger man."

Chapter 10

PENELOPE

A muted glow seeps from beneath the blinds and fills the room with an unexpected amount of warmth. And when I roll over, and remember the body beside me, I wonder if it's more than the sun that's making me feel this way.

Last night was absolute bliss.

If it had been any better, I would've thought I'd died and gone to heaven.

The sex was just that good. Scratch that, everything about Cord is just that good.

I turn so I can quietly slip out of bed when an arm hooks across my waist and drags me back.

"Where do you think you're going?" Cord buries his head between my shoulder and my neck, pressing his lips against my skin.

I push against him, my naked back curled into his naked front. "I thought you were asleep. I didn't want to wake you."

"If you're awake," he starts while one of his hands curls around my hip and slips in between my legs. The other slides between the bed and my body until he's cupping my breast. "Then I'm awake."

I place each of my hands over his. “Are you enjoying yourself?” I tease.

He pushes a finger inside of me, and I gasp in surprise.

“If you think there is a single part of me that *isn’t* spending the weekend inside of you, then maybe last night wasn’t as good for you as it was for me.”

He adds another finger, and I can’t help but wonder what it would be like to wake up this needy and feeling so wanted by this man, everyday of your life. It’s a delicious ache knowing that another person’s only mission is to satiate you.

He drops open-mouthed kisses all down my neck, shoulder, and back as he continues to fuck me with his fingers. His other hand kneads my breast, occasionally tweaking my nipple.

“I need to be inside you,” he growls.

He’s about to move, when I throw my arm back and keep him in place. “Like this,” I breathe. “Fuck me just like this.”

I feel like a different person, initiating sex, making requests and actually having them listened to. It’s been such a long time since the pleasure was all mine.

Cord widens my legs and accurately angles his hips. He swaps his fingers for his cock and I moan when I feel him push all the way inside me.

I turn my head to face him and he captures my lips in an act of pure desperation. My tongue tastes him with just as much fervor as he thrusts in and out of me.

Groans and moans echo around the room as we continue to get lost in one another.

“I just want to live here,” he murmurs against my lips while bringing a finger to my throbbing clit. “I want to feel your pussy around me all day long.”

I whimper at just the idea of us having access to one

another all day, every day. To having him inside me whenever I wanted, to be inundated with so much lust and so many feelings.

He rocks his hips, harder and faster, and I feel myself climbing that familiar peak.

"Cord," I pant. "I... I... I..."

"I know, baby. Let me get you there."

With his fingers rolling my clit and teasing my nipples, and his cock relentlessly pounding into me, I feel myself fall off unimaginable heights of pleasure and dive right into an abyss I don't ever want to come out of.

"There you go," he soothes. His voice is so soft and relaxing, but his body is not.

He grabs himself out of me and orders, "Get on all fours."

Even though I'm a little wobbly, I do as he says. When my ass is in the air, he slaps it and then slams into me from behind.

He grips my hips, stopping me from jerking forward, and relentlessly fucks me. It doesn't take long for the need in my body to reignite and another orgasm to ripple through me. But this time, I feel Cord lose himself inside me. His cock pulsing, his come filling me up.

Any inhibitions either of us had, or any reservations between us, no longer exist. Each time we're intimate, it's more poignant and meaningful than the times before.

Still inside me, Cord softly presses his mouth on each shoulder and gently down my spine.

"Let me clean you up," he says in between kisses.

And I do. For the first time in a long time, I let a man take care of me.

We're tangled up together on the couch, sharing popcorn like high school lovers, and it reminds me of all the reasons being alone isn't as fun as I initially thought it would be.

Cord has to go back to Ted's tomorrow and I'm trying not to get caught up in my feelings about it.

Instead, I flip the focus of the night to Cord and his life before Merlot, hoping it provides the reminder I need to not let myself get attached to someone who's going to leave.

And as he should, because what twenty-one-year-old wants to settle down in wine country with a thirty-three-year-old woman?

"Do you ever think of the night of your accident?" I ask him.

He stills at the question, not irritated or annoyed but more surprised. He finds the remote and presses pause on the movie.

"I definitely think about how stupid I was," he answers. "Sometimes, I try to remember exactly why I got behind the wheel in the first place. Like, what compelled me to go along with something I *know* is dangerous?"

"You don't seem like you have any answers to those questions," I say sadly.

He shakes his head. "I don't. But I feel lucky to be alive. Lucky to be here with you."

I feel the same way but don't elaborate, because there's nothing more to say. Nothing more that can be said besides three little words that I can imagine myself saying to someone like Cord if we were given the time to be something more than a 'summer fling'.

"Was it out of character for you to drink and drive?" I query.

A hint of shame appears on his face. "I'm a risk-taker. A

go-getter by nature. So it's not unusual for me to take a ride on the wild side and not think of the consequences."

I concentrate on anything but him when I ask, "Is that what this is for you? A ride on the wild side, having sex with an older woman?"

"Pen." I know he wants my attention. The nickname out of his mouth, comfortable and endearing. When he repeats my name, I look up at him. "What do you want this to be for me?" he asks.

"I don't know," I say honestly. "I guess I just hope when you go back home that you'll still remember me." *Because I don't think I'll ever forget you.*

Cupping my cheeks, he brings my mouth to his. "You're impossible to forget."

He could be placating me or he could be telling the truth. Either way, I let those words sink beneath my skin and kiss him.

"You want to go again?" he asks.

I pull back and peer up at him. "You're serious?"

"I thought I made it very clear how much sex we were going to have."

"You did," I assure him. "But I didn't really expect your dick to actually deliver."

"Oh, is that so?" he scoffs. He grabs one of my hands and brings it to his hardening dick. "Ready, each and every time, baby." The smirk on his face is wicked and I absolutely love it.

I start to massage him when his hand stops me. "Want to go out for dessert?"

"Now?" I ask. "It won't be worth it to drive out of town this late at night."

"Why don't we just have dessert *in* town."

"Anyone could see us." As soon as the words leave my mouth, I know I've upset him.

"Is it such a big deal to be seen with me?"

"No, it's just..."

"It's just what?" he presses.

"Everyone will know what we're doing together."

"You think everyone doesn't already know what we're doing together? You think they don't see me go into your store every fucking morning? I'm not buying clothes, Penelope."

I try to ignore his logic, more infuriated by his accurate assessment of the situation. I guess in my mind, always eating out of town and sneaking into the shop before everything else opened up meant we were safe.

"And what if someone tells Ted," I add, knowing someone *will* tell him. "What will we say to him?"

"How about trying the truth," he deadpans.

I raise an eyebrow at him.

"Okay, how about we're just two consenting adults enjoying each other's company."

It's the truth and it's simple, but it's naive to think it will go down exactly like that. Without a problem. Without a hitch.

Choosing not to dwell on it, I give in. "You really want to go out for dessert?"

"I really want to *take you out* for dessert," he clarifies. "I want you to dress up in one of those short dresses you wear. Slip into some heels and then let me feed you ice cream and seduce you with chocolate."

"And then?"

"And then we're going to come back home and I'm going to have you for dessert." I press my legs together, already turned on by his verbal foreplay. "I'm going to fuck you into the early morning. Fuck you until you're nothing but a quivering mess who can't think of sex without thinking of me."

"Do we really need to go out for dessert?" I ask breathlessly, my arousal evident in my voice.

He slaps my ass. "Yes. I promise the wait will be worth it."

Chapter 11

CORD

Leaving Penelope at work this morning to come to the station was difficult, but knowing I'm going back as soon as my shift ends helps. I've been walking around all day with a permanent smile on my face. For the first time ever, I've got the world by the balls and it feels amazing. Work is going well, I'm staying out of trouble, and I'm head over heels for Penelope. Life is everything I've always hoped it would be and more.

I don't even miss being at the house I grew up in. My parents have made it clear they're not going to have much to do with me. It makes me sad, especially that my mom is following my dad's directives. I know no matter how upset she is with me, it's not like her to not speak with me every few days. I can't control how they act, so I'm focusing on what I need to and figuring out what makes me happy. And that's spending time with Penelope.

I'm also really enjoying my time at the police station. Working there has solidified my plans to become a police officer. If I end up being in the Merlot Department, even better. I've come to love this place like it's always been my home, and I don't want to leave, even when it's time to return to school.

I finish mopping the bathroom floors and return the bucket and mop to the supply closet. I wander down the long hall and knock on the doorway to Lieutenant Gardner's office.

He lifts his eyes from his laptop screen. "Renner, what can I do for you?"

"Nothing at all. I just wanted to take a minute to thank you for giving me this opportunity. I love working here." I smile.

"You're a good toilet cleaner, that's for sure. Maybe the best one we've had." He grins. "It's been a pleasure having you here. You're a hard worker and you don't complain. Both of those qualities are things I value in an employee."

"Thank you, Lieutenant." Pressing my lips together for a moment, I try to decide if I should voice my concerns or not. But if I don't ask Lieutenant Gardner, I'll probably never get the opportunity to ask anyone else. "If I finish college and don't get into any more trouble, do you think it's possible I'd be able to become a police officer?"

"It won't be an easy path like it would be if you didn't have a history of misbehaving, but it's possible. Stay focused on your studies and keep your head down. You'll do great."

"Thank you, Lieutenant. I appreciate your honesty. I'm done for the night. I'll see you tomorrow."

"Night, Renner."

Exiting the front door, I jog down the stairs, coming to an abrupt halt when I see Uncle Ted leaning against the passenger side of his car. I smile through my disappointment. It's not that I'm not happy to see him. After our shared car ride the other morning, I think we're in a great place, but

I was supposed to ride with Penelope back to her house. I walk over to him. "Hey, how was your weekend?"

"It was exactly what I expected it to be." He seems so serious. Maybe he's tired.

"Are you on your way home?" I ask.

"No, *we're* on our way home," he replies.

"I'm not sure what you mean. Do you want me to come back to the house and help you with something?"

"Is there a reason why you need to be out?" he questions.

"No. Let's get going."

He moves around his car and slips into the driver's seat. I throw a final longing-filled glance across the street at Penelope's store and climb inside the car. *Fuck.* Ideally, this is the point where I should tell him I've got plans with Penelope, but I can't. Once he knows we're involved, he'll shut down any chance of us being together. It doesn't matter that I'm an adult. I'm staying under his roof and paying him back for his help.

As much as I'd like to put my foot down, I can't just walk away from my obligation. If I did, I'd be no better than I was before I arrived. I'm working on becoming a better person, not just for me but for my family. And now Penelope is part of that equation too. I don't want to do anything that will disappoint her.

I type out a text to Penelope.

Me: Hey, my uncle showed up at the station and needed me to go home with him. Not sure why, but I'll fill you in as soon as I know.

My phone vibrates with her reply.

Penelope: No worries. I'm sorry I won't get to see you, but I'll just make up for it tomorrow. xo

I smile before typing my reply.

Me: I'm going to hold you to it—literally.

Penelope: Ha ha. That better be a promise.

Me: Oh, it is.

"Who are you texting that has you so happy? Is there a girl I should know about?" Uncle Ted asks, making me aware that I've completely forgotten I'm in the car with him. Penelope has the ability to take my focus from everything but her. But I guess that's what being in love is all about. Damn. I finally admit the depth of my feelings to myself and I'm in the car with my uncle of all places.

"No, there's no girl," I reply. Actually, she's a beautiful woman.

"Are you sure? I recognize that look. I've seen it on Leon's face enough times." Whatever my expression showed, comparing it to Leon's meaningless and frequent crushes is an insult. Obviously I can't tell uncle Ted this.

"Yeah, I'm sure. It's a female friend from back home. We're not romantically interested in each other."

"You may find once you're home that things have changed. When you spend time apart, feelings can shift. Sometimes it's for the better and sometimes it's for the worse."

I'm not sure what he's getting at, but since it's Penelope I've been sharing texts with, it's irrelevant.

The ride home is quick, and once we're inside the house, I expect him to ask me for help with something.

"Hand me your phone," he orders.

"What?" I ask, certain I've misheard.

"Hand your phone to me, now." This time he's louder and more commanding.

"No." I shake my head. "Why do you want my phone?"

"Your parents asked me to take it from you since they're the ones footing the bill."

Where is this coming from? Why are they asking for my

phone when I've been here for over a month? It makes no sense.

"I'm waiting," he reminds me, his hand extended.

Fuck me. I place my phone in his palm and frown when he drops it in the pocket on his suit pants.

"When can I have that back?" I ask.

"That's up to your parents. I need you to go pack up your things. They want you home for a few days." His words stir up panic inside me.

"Did something happen to one of them? Are they sick or hurt?"

"No, they're fine. Go get your stuff. I'll be driving you home tonight."

"But you must be exhausted after your trip." I'm desperate to delay my leaving.

"I feel surprisingly awake." He glances at the platinum watch on his wrist. "We're leaving in ten minutes. Your mom said to bring everything home, so she can make sure you have everything you need for school."

"That doesn't make sense."

"She mentioned you might not need as much stuff here since the summer is half over."

"Yeah, that makes sense. I brought a bunch of extra shit."

"Okay, get going. We need to hit the road."

"Why can't we wait until tomorrow?" I ask.

"Because your parents asked me to bring you tonight."

I rake a hand through my hair, my frustration evident, before I climb the stairs. My clothes and everything else I brought gets shoved into my duffel bags. Taking a final glance around the room, I make sure I'm not forgetting anything. I never thought I'd be sad to leave here, but I am. Luckily, I'll be returning in a few days.

I hope Penelope won't worry when she doesn't hear from

me tonight. With any luck, once I'm home, I can talk my parents into letting me have my phone back.

UNCLE TED STAYS quiet for the first half of the trip, allowing me to drift off to sleep. When I wake and see where I am, I realize this wasn't a bad dream after all. *Shit.*

"How long have you and Penelope been seeing one another?" My head snaps toward uncle Ted. "You didn't think anyone would find out?" he asks, and I stay silent. "You can admit what was going on. I know. Others know too. Even your parents."

"Is that the real reason you're bringing me home?"

"Yes. Your parents are very concerned with your situation and wanted you removed from it as soon as possible." My heart races as the realization of what's really happening hits.

"It's not a situation."

"What do you think it is?"

"A relationship."

He barks out a laugh. "You think a woman like Penelope would fall for someone like you?" he scoffs.

"I don't just think it, I know she did."

"Don't be so naive, Cord. Penelope is a successful businesswoman. Her tastes are better suited to someone older and equally successful."

"Someone like you, you mean?" I chuckle. "Yeah, too bad she friend zoned you. I guess you don't know her as well as you seem to think you do. It seems she prefers the younger Renner."

"For the time being," he goads.

"Stay the fuck away from her," I order, my anger stirring.

"She'll need a man's shoulder to cry on. I can be that for her. It won't take long for her to forget about you. Summer flings always end."

"We weren't a fling," I grit out.

"Are you sure about that?" he taunts.

"I'm done talking about this with you." Leaning my temple against the glass, I close my eyes and do my best to calm my temper. I want to punch out the window beneath my head. Drawing up Penelope's face in my mind, I recall the special way she has of looking at me. It's like she notices parts of me no one else does. Even if she's not ready to reveal her feelings, she still makes me feel loved.

Chapter 12

PENELOPE

He's gone?

He's gone?

He's gone.

I don't know why I keep questioning it when it's actual fact. It's been a full week, and I need to start coming to terms with the fact that he's no longer here.

When he didn't text back to tell me why Ted picked him up, my chest tightened in worry. When I stopped by the station and asked Paul if he'd shown up, he told me Ted had advised him that Cord was needed back at home for a family emergency. At that, I just knew in my gut him leaving had nothing to do with his family needing him, and everything to do with our relationship.

Every morning, I keep telling myself I can do this, that I need to forget he ever existed and go back to being the recently divorced woman who is all about finding her independence. But by the time I drag myself to bed, alone, every night, I realize I'm nothing more than a woman who is destined to always be consumed by feelings of loss, hopelessness, and heartache.

Frustrated, I pace up and down the shop, trying to make sense of how we went from having a perfect weekend to me nursing a broken heart over my twenty-one-year-old fuck buddy.

Even the errant thought makes me flinch. He is so much more than a fuck buddy, and this emptiness in my chest only solidifies it.

It wasn't supposed to be this way. I wasn't supposed to want him for more than a fling, and it wasn't supposed to hurt this much to know he's gone.

I call his cell again, feeling an overwhelming sense of craziness trying to get in touch with him, but the call doesn't go through.

It never goes through.

There's only one person I know who will give me the answers I need, and yet I still can't face him.

It's that stupid voice inside my head that keeps telling me this meant more to me than Cord. That stupid voice in my head that reminds me that I repeatedly told him it wouldn't amount to anything because he was leaving. So he did exactly what I told him to do and left.

But a month early?

There's something at the pit of my stomach that doesn't sit right. He may have always been leaving, but there was no reason he would need to cut contact. Not so abruptly. Not so harshly.

Even a "break-up" message over text would've sufficed at a time like this. But this silence is completely uncharacteristic. And even after only knowing him for a month, I'm absolutely certain of that.

My phone rings and I reluctantly pick it up.

"Hey."

"Are we still moping?" Delia asks.

I try to perk up. I try not to fall into the same bad habits I fell into when Eric and I were having trouble. Because I don't want to push her away this time, nor do I want to resurrect and drown in old feelings of shame and embarrassment.

I was with a guy and it didn't work out. It's that simple. At least it feels like it should be that simple.

"No," I supply through a weak smile. "I'm much better this week."

"You're the worst liar, Pen."

"I'm not lying," I argue. "This is nothing like what happened between Eric and me."

"Just because it's not the same doesn't mean it hurts any less."

Tears well in my eyes at her empathy. "I feel like I'm going crazy," I whisper. "I should've never jumped into something so soon."

"How were you supposed to know you were going to fall in love with the guy?"

Fall in love? Is that what this is? Did I fall in love with Cord?

"Pen." The tone in Delia's voice changes. She's more serious now, the sympathy nowhere to be found.

"Yeah?"

"Why won't you go and ask Ted what happened?"

It's a valid question. Logical even.

"I'm scared," I confess.

"Of Ted?" she asks, her voice rising in concern

"No. Not of *him* specifically. But, I just..."

"You just?"

"I should've known he would find out," I say, steering the conversation in an opposite direction. "He showed up at the shop knowing to look for Cord there. It was stupid to think we could keep it a secret here or that people wouldn't notice."

"Didn't Ted ask you to keep an eye on Cord anyway?" she asks, trying to untangle the mess that is my train of thought.

"I'm sure he meant in more of a friend type of way. An older sister, maybe?"

"Well, that assumption is on him. His problem. Not yours."

"So you don't think I did the wrong thing? Took advantage of the situation? Betrayed Ted's trust?"

"Oh my god," she gasps. "Is that what this is? The reason you're avoiding Ted?"

"We were friends, Delia," I say solemnly. "He clearly doesn't think too much of me now."

"Penelope," she reprimands. "That is not how this is going to go. You will not get your heart broken and then concern yourself with the thoughts and feelings of those who caused you pain."

She's right. I know she's right. If Ted is the reason all this went down, then he wasn't the friend I thought he was anyway. Who cares what he thinks of me? His opinion does not outweigh my happiness.

"You're right. You're absolutely right," I say to Delia. "I'm going to see Ted," I exclaim. "I'm going to get to the bottom of this shit. Because if Cord wants us broken up, then I'm going to make him say it to my face."

Delia squeals in my ear. "Rip that motherfucker a new asshole, Pen Pen," she cheers. "He fucking deserves it."

I don't know if she means Cord or Ted, but I guess in the right context either could work.

"Thank you," I say to my best friend. "Thank you for being you."

"I love you, Pen."

"I love you too."

HOPING OUT OF MY CAR, I walk straight into Ted's office and smile at Janine, who is extremely confused to see me. Or maybe she's just playing dumb. Considering the whole town's talking about Cord and me, I wouldn't be surprised if she expected me to show up at some point.

"How can I help you today, Penelope?" Janine greets politely.

"Is Ted in?" I ask a little too sweetly. "I wasn't able to get an appointment, but I really need to see him."

Before she has a chance to speak to him, his office door is already opening. He steps out with a client of his, but his eyes land on me almost immediately.

He peruses my body, something I very much anticipated when I dressed up to kill.

Reluctantly, he drags his gaze away from me and says his goodbyes to the older man.

I keep my stance casual and my facial expression neutral as I wait. When Ted eventually, wordlessly guides me into his office and closes the door, I pounce.

"Tell me what happened," I demand.

He slowly turns to face me, acting cool and calm, but the slight clenching of his jaw gives his true feelings away.

"I'm sorry," he says. "I wasn't aware you and I had an appointment."

"Don't play dumb, Ted. Tell me about Cord. Tell me why he left."

"He didn't tell you? I would assume if you two were in an

actual relationship, then he would've told you," he says sarcastically.

"THIS ISN'T FUNNY, TED," I say, feeling disheartened. "I need to speak to Cord."

As if he's ignoring my requests, he continues to walk across the office and doesn't stop till he's seated at his desk.

"You were supposed to watch out for him," he says cooly. "You weren't supposed to fuck him."

I straighten my spine and let his hostility wash over me. Knowing he was going to say this versus actually hearing it changes my whole demeanor. Because in my mind, it would be said with disgust and repulsion, but here, in this office, the only thing I can hear is his jealousy.

"Mad it wasn't you, Ted? Did I bruise your ego a little, so you thought you'd hurt me back?" He watches me as I walk toward him, his face telling me nothing. In a few strides, I'm at his desk and take the seat in the leather chair across from him. "I thought we were friends," I say softly.

"I thought you didn't want to date after the divorce," he counters. "But I guess you really didn't want to date me."

"It wasn't personal, Ted," I reassure him, hoping this softer tone between us gives me the answers I need to get to speak to Cord. "I didn't plan on being with or falling for anyone."

"You love him?" he asks quickly.

"I think so," I answer honestly. "I haven't known him for long, but he's changed me, Ted, and I won't walk away from that. And if I have to explain it to you and everybody else who is so quick to judge us, then that's what I'm going to do."

"And what if his parents don't want you around him?" he asks, hoping to deter me.

"Well, I guess they're going to have to decide which outcome they can live with more. Hating me or Cord hating them."

"I wouldn't hold your breath, princess," he says condescendingly. "That boy is used to a life of privilege that both you and your magical pussy won't be able to keep up with."

I ignore his words, knowing he's just trying to make it sting. Trying to goad me.

"Tell me how to reach him, Ted," I ask for the last time

"You're going to regret this," he warns. "He's going to let you down."

I shake my head at him vehemently, hating the disregard he has for Cord's feelings and his inability to see that the only person who can't be trusted in this situation is him. He played Cord's parents, knowing if he made our relationship out to sound horrible they would side with him and then bring Cord home. And then he'd be here to swoop in and pick up the pieces of what's left of me.

"For the record, Ted," I say, preparing to add insult to injury. "Even without Cord in the picture, I wouldn't pick you."

Even though his face is beet red and his nostrils are flaring, he grabs the closest legal pad and scribbles on it. He tears off the paper and hands it to me. It's got an address and a number on it.

Yes.

My body buzzes in elation. I'm finally going to be able to see Cord.

I shove the paper in my bag, just as he says, "It's okay, I don't want his sloppy seconds now anyway."

Choosing to ignore the bait, I hold Ted's stare and exhale

loudly. He doesn't deserve my niceties, and I refuse to stoop his level.

I am better than him.

Cord is better than him.

"Thank you, Ted." Confusion mars his features, and just like the lawyer he is, I see the way he's itching for my comeback. Itching for that fight. I offer him a soft smile instead. "I'll tell your family you said hi."

Chapter 13

CORD

It's been days since arriving back home, and my parents and I have done a great job at ignoring one another. There seems to be so much to talk about, but I can't even stand to look at either of them. I just need to speak to Penelope.

Knowing my phone has to be here somewhere, I drag myself out of my bedroom and start to look for it in all my parents' favorite hiding places.

When the only place that's left is my dad's office, I hold my breath and take the plunge.

The room is nothing but a mash-up of my father's favorite things. Nothing about the way the items are displayed makes sense to anyone but him. My father loves to make sure that his collections are visible for all to see, and this place is his area to do so.

I head to his desk and begin to rummage through his drawers. By the time I'm through, the only option I have left is to try and crack the code to his safe. I feel like I'm in a movie, because my mind is yet to fully comprehend why they care about me and Penelope. Apart from sending me to Merlot in the first place, this is the only other time my parents have exerted their authority and it doesn't even make sense. What's worse is their "punishment" and decision to take away all the technology in the house seems like the type of punishment you'd give a sixteen-year-old kid, not a grown twenty-one-year-old.

Every combination falls short, and I'm just about to give up when I hear a soft click. I pull open the heavy door and see my phone and laptop sitting on the top shelf. Quickly, I pull them out, place them on my father's desk and fire them both up.

My hands are shaky as I type in passwords and wait for my cell to power up. The sliver of excitement coursing through me stills when I see a set up screen on both of my devices.

"We wiped them clean." My father's voice startles me, but it's the words that come out of his mouth that crush me.

I turn to look at him while that little voice in my head tells me this isn't the end of the world, I will eventually get back to her. No matter how many roadblocks they want to throw my way.

"What the hell were you thinking?" Before I can answer, he cuts me off. "I know, you weren't thinking. You never do." He shakes his head, disgusted with me.

"I love her," I confess to him, hating that it isn't Penelope who's hearing me say it for the first time. "This isn't some meaningless fling."

As if she'd been eavesdropping outside, my mom comes in with a sympathetic look on her face. "Honey, she's too old to be involved with. You're just starting your life, and she's already been divorced once. She's probably latched herself on to you because you have money and her biological clock is ticking."

"Mom, none of that is even close to being the truth. The

age difference doesn't matter, not when you love someone. And if she wants to have kids with me, then I'll give her a whole football team."

"Honey." She shakes her head in pity. "Believe me, the age difference does matter. It will become a problem later on."

"Have you had a relationship with a younger man?" I ask.

She looks shocked. "No. Of course not."

"Then why should I believe you when you have no experience in this matter?"

"It doesn't matter anyway," my dad barks, finally joining in on the conversation. "You're here and she's there. And you'll continue to abide by our rules until you return to school. That includes no phone and internet."

"I'm twenty-one," I protest. "And I need to call her."

"While you're under our roof, you'll respect our goddamn wishes," he shouts. Clenching my fists, I step forward until we're chest to chest. "You better check yourself, son, or you'll be out on your ass before you know what hit you," he tells me.

The urge to hit him is so powerful, I have to turn and walk away. This is my father, and no matter how angry I am, I won't strike him. I keep moving until I reach my room and throw myself down on the bed. Thoughts of Penelope and a plan to get to her consume my thoughts. What is she thinking? How angry is she that I left without saying goodbye? Does she know this wasn't by choice? Has she tried to contact me? Does she know I love her?

My eyes sting with tears and I scrub my hands up and down my face. I won't allow myself to cry. Instead, I turn my thoughts to what I need to do before I start back at college.

"I FOUND A JOB," I inform my parents at dinner a week later. It's been almost two weeks since I was dragged away from Merlot, and this is how every exchange between me and my parents has been.

There's little to no emotion. No love lost, no love gained. I might as well be asking for the bowl of corn to be passed to me.

"Doing what?" my mom asks.

"Working security at the hospital."

"How did you get that job?" Dad asks.

"One of my friend's uncles is the head of security there. I guess they're short staffed with so many people taking summer vacations. My buddy and I are both going to work there for the next couple of weeks."

"I'm not sure you should be working. I don't need you out all hours of the night."

No, they both want me to be like a prisoner here, and I've been letting them get away with it while I bide my time and slowly set my plan into motion.

The only problem is, I need money. I need money for a car, I need money to get away from them. And I need it soon. I won't shy away from hard work, I never have.

And for Penelope, I'll do just about anything.

"I'll be home whenever I don't have a shift."

"I want to see your schedule ahead of time. No springing shifts on us last minute," Dad tells me.

"Okay. That shouldn't be a problem." Ducking my head, I shove a forkful of mashed potatoes into my mouth to hide my smile. I'm feeling hopeful for the first time since I left Merlot.

I'm just about to fall asleep on the couch when the doorbell rings. Without my cell nearby, I assume it's about eight thirty at night, which is somewhat late for unexpected visitors at my parents' place.

At first, I think it's my parents, since they went to run a quick errand after dinner, but that's stupid because they have a key.

It rings again, and I lazily rise up off the couch and, without urgency, walk to the door.

Opening it with no expectations, I'm absolutely stunned to see a nervous looking Penelope on the other side.

14

PENELOPE

PENELOPE

When I decided to make the long drive to see Cord, I told myself to lower my expectations and pretty much prepare for the worst. I told myself he might not want me, and he might've not missed me at all.

But I knew I needed to see him. I needed to know the decisions made to end us were his. I needed to hear it from the horse's mouth, no matter how much that was going to hurt.

"Penelope." His eyes are wide with shock, almost like the idea of me being at his house never even occurred to him. "What are you doing here?"

I nervously wring my hands together. "Should I not be here?"

My question seems to shake him out of his stupor and he rushes at me, his hands grabbing my face, his mouth descending on mine.

The tension that I've been holding for the last two weeks disintegrates into dust when his lips touch mine. It's like the fog has been lifted and the blanket of doubt and insecurities can finally be tucked away.

"I can't believe you're actually here," he murmurs. "At my house."

Unable to keep his hands off me, he continues to kiss and touch me in the doorway.

Eventually, we move inside, our mouths still meshed together. He guides us down a long hallway and then we have to part when he opens the door. When we're in his bedroom, his lips are back on mine, as if he needs to kiss me to breathe.

I don't want him to stop. Not now. Not ever. But this is his parents' house, and from what I've gathered, I'm almost certain they will not be pleased with my arrival.

Pushing at his chest, I pull away from him reluctantly.

"What's wrong?" He frowns.

"I don't want to get carried away in your parents' house," I tell him. "And we need to talk."

"What's there to talk about?" His words surprise me.

"How about why you left? If you're coming back? What that means for us?" I slap a hand across my mouth, because I told myself no expectations and *this* is not *that*. "I'm sorry," I say sheepishly.

He chuckles and then wraps his arms around me, his chin resting on my head. "I thought it would be ages before I would get to hold you again," he says.

I squeeze him tighter, not wanting to let him go. Letting myself finally feel just how much I missed him.

"I missed you," I whisper into his chest. "I missed you so much."

"Come lie down with me," he suggests.

I look up at him. "No sex in your parents' house."

He laughs, and the sound warms me from the inside out. "No sex in my parents' house," he assures me.

Tangled up in one another, Cord tells me what happened the night Ted picked him up.

How angry he was and how angry his parents were.

"I honestly didn't see it coming," he admits. "I know they have a problem with almost everything I do, but this was a whole other side of them I'd never seen. They wiped my cell. They wiped my laptop. It was completely unnecessary."

"I guess that explains why I couldn't get in touch with you and why you never called."

He rests a palm on my cheek, his thumb brushing my cheekbone. "In the first few days I was irate, trying to get in touch with you. But they watched me like a hawk. Like I was in danger of hurting them or myself. And then when I found out they tried to erase every single last remnant of you, I just knew I had to move my focus to something else."

"What do you mean?" I ask.

"I was going crazy not being able to talk to you," he explains. "But trying to get them to see reason was useless, and I realized I just needed to get back to you as quickly as possible and the rest of it would fall into place."

A lone tear falls out of the corner of my eye. "You've always been so sure about us."

He wipes another stray tear. "I'll be sure enough for the both of us for as long as I need to be."

"What were you going to do when you got back to me?"

His eyes soften, and for the first time ever, Cord Renner looks a little shy. "I was going to tell you I love you."

I open my mouth to say something, but he puts a finger on my lips, silencing me. "Let me finish." I watch his Adam's apple bob in his throat as he tries to compose himself. "I was going to tell you that I love you. That I'm in love with you. I was going to thank you for seeing me for the man I am and the man I want to be and not judging me for all my past mistakes. And I was going to see if your bed needed warming at night, because I'm going to need a place to live when I move back to Merlot with you."

My infrequent tears now turn into two consistent streams running down my face. He's so open with his feelings. Honest and brave, and I want to be that with him too.

"What about your life here?" I ask.

"You're not here," he answers matter-of-factly. "I don't want to be anywhere you're not."

Struggling to hold the words inside any longer, I blurt the three words out in a wonderful sigh of relief. "I love you, Cord Renner."

He smiles down at me and tilts his head before kissing me. "I love you too."

Despite my reservations about sex in his parents' house, it isn't enough to deter me from kissing him the way I want to. It isn't enough to stop me from pouring my heart into his, or from tasting all the promises we will make to one another or the possibilities our life together will have. We kiss away the sadness and welcome our new beginnings with every stroke of our tongues.

I know this is the start of what will be an uneasy road for

Cord. Moving his whole life. Choosing a life with me at the cost of potentially losing his family. It's a bittersweet happy ever after, but he's everything I didn't know I wanted, and everything I don't want to live without.

"We'll make it work," he whispers into my mouth. "I promise."

Epilogue

CORD

FIVE YEARS LATER

I often wondered if this day would ever come, and now that it's here, it seems surreal. I just graduated from the Police Academy and I am officially a member of the Merlot Police force. I have everything I've ever wanted. I'm not sure how I got so lucky, but I'm going to spend every single day being grateful for my many blessings. Especially the two beauties walking toward me now.

Catching Penelope's eye, I smile. My eighteen-month-old daughter, Cordelia—yes she's named after me and Penelope's best friend Delia—reaches for me.

"Da Da up." I steal a quick kiss from Penelope before taking Cordelia from her.

Who can resist so much cuteness? Definitely not me. I'm a big softie when it comes to her. I know I need to curb my tendency to give her whatever she wants, but it's so damn hard. When she smiles and looks up at me with green eyes so much like my own, my chest aches from the abundance of love I feel for her.

Brushing her black curls back from her eyes, I press a kiss to her forehead.

"Tell Daddy congratulations," Penelope says.

"Grat uns, Da Da."

"Thank you, my little baby girl."

"Congratulations, Cord. I'm so proud of you," Penelope says. I can see the pride shining in her eyes. We've both been waiting for this day to come. It took longer than I would've liked, but even with the extra steps along the path, I still got here.

"Cord, I'm so proud of you." My mom hurries over to hug me. She kisses Cordelia's pink cheek. "Grammy loves you."

My dad steps in and hooks his arms around his granddaughter, forcing me to hand her over. "Give me my girl." He makes silly faces at her and she giggles. He pats me on the back. "Congratulations, son. You did great. I'm proud of you."

"Thank you, Dad. That means a lot." His long awaited words choke me up. It took us until Cordelia was born for my dad to really understand how much Penelope and I love one another and how committed to our relationship we are.

When we got pregnant, my parents were upset because we weren't married and didn't have plans to be any time soon. But Penelope and I have been together for over five years now. We're as good as married as far we're concerned. I'd marry her tomorrow if she was ready, but after her first marriage ended in divorce, she wanted to try the untraditional route.

And how could I argue with her? After all, our relationship is considered untraditional by most people. I seem to have a history of doing things differently. I used to wonder what was wrong with me, why I couldn't be like everyone else. But now I accept all the craziness in my past and I'm thankful I got it out of my system.

Another bonus to my dark past, Cordelia won't get away with anything when she's a teenager.

"Cord." Uncle Ted calls my name. He pulls me in for a back-slapping hug. He's another family member who finally accepted that Penelope and I are meant to be together. Not that she or I were particularly concerned if he or other people weren't accepting of us. We knew early on that our love is the kind that endures forever. If others didn't agree, we figured they'd learn for themselves over time.

"Uncle Ted, it's great to see you."

"Congratulations. You deserve this."

"Thank you. It means a lot that you think so." I glance around, searching for my cousin. "Where's Leon?"

"He's busy talking with all the single women."

I jab his arm with the point of my elbow. "Like father, like son."

He grins. "I feel like I should be thanking you for steering him in the right direction. I never imagined he'd want to be a police officer."

"No need to thank me. Besides, I think it's awesome we're starting our careers together. Maybe we'll even end up as partners someday."

"Oh, Jesus. This town isn't ready for that," he says. "At least wait until I retire and move away."

"I don't know. It might be exactly what this town needs. And who are you kidding? You're not going anywhere."

"I can dream can't I?" Uncle Ted jokes.

"Nothing wrong with dreaming big. It didn't hurt me any." I look over at Penelope and find her watching me with appraising eyes. "If you'll excuse me, Uncle Ted. I need to catch up with Penelope."

"Is that what you call it?" He winks.

"Something like that," I say before walking away.

Penelope's interest grows as I approach, her gaze running over me from head to toe and back up again.

Stopping when we're toe-to-toe, I lean down and whisper in her ear, "It's the uniform isn't it?" Straightening up to my full height, I puff my chest out and hold still for her to objectify.

"It's you, but the uniform isn't hurting any."

"What do you say we get out of here and head home. It'll be time for Cordelia to go to sleep and it'll be time for us to go to bed." I wink.

"I think it's a great idea, but it means prying Cordelia from your dad's arms."

"Leave that to me."

WHEN WE ARRIVED at our home, the same split level Penelope had just moved into when we met, she told me to leave my uniform on. I guess she really does like it.

We fed Cordelia her dinner, changed her into her pajamas, and tucked her into bed. Penelope is lingering outside her room to make sure she's going to sleep. She recently climbed out of her crib for the first time and now every night, we wait for it to happen again.

I'm sitting on the end of the mattress in our room when Penelope walks in. She smiles. "She went out like a little angel."

"She'll save the climbing shenanigans for when we're asleep," I say.

"Probably. She is your daughter," Penelope drolls, sauntering toward me. If I'm not mistaken, she adds extra wiggle to her hips.

"Which means she's destined to be awesome?" I lean back, bracing my hands behind me on the mattress.

"Mmhmm," she agrees, but it sounds more skeptical than anything else. She stops, standing between my legs, and drops to her knees. My next breath catches in my chest. Is this going where I hope it is?

Penelope runs her hands up and down my thighs. "I'm always proud to be with you, but today I can't put into words the pride I felt. You worked so hard to achieve this and had to be patient. You deserve every bit of success, and I know you're going to be an amazing police officer."

"Thank you. I always want you to be proud of me."

"I always am."

"God, I love you," I tell her.

"I love you too."

I tuck a strand of her hair behind her ear. "And for the record, *we* worked so hard to achieve this. It was a team effort."

"That's sweet of you to say, but you did all the heavy lifting. Now, no more disagreeing with me. I've got a better idea."

"If your idea is what I hope it is, this really is the best day of my life."

"Oh, it's going there, for sure." Her fingers are quick to undo my belt.

"You like seeing me in my uniform, huh?" She gets my pants unfastened. "Or maybe it's the handcuffs?" I raise my hips, and she tugs my pants and boxer briefs down to my thighs. "Or is it the gun?"

She grips my cock, squeezing. "It's this gun."

I groan. "Watch out. It's loaded and there's a bullet in the chamber."

"There's only one place this gun is going off." Leaning forward, she wraps her lips around the head of my cock and slides all the way down until I'm bumping the back of her throat.

"Oh, Christ." My fingers sink into her long, black hair as she begins to bob up and down. This woman is one of a kind. I can't believe she's real and she's all mine. "Don't stop," I husk, and she hums. I fall to my back on the bed, surrendering to the ecstasy radiating from my groin.

Penelope has an exceptionally talented mouth, and I'm fighting off my orgasm so one, this won't end yet, and two, I can get inside her before I explode.

With hands on each side of Penelope's head, I tug her from my cock. "I want you riding my cock when I blow."

Scrambling to her feet, she yanks her dress up to her waist and her panties to the floor where she kicks them aside. I back up farther onto the mattress, giving her room to straddle my lap. Gripping my cock, she guides me to her warm, wet entrance and slides down my length like a fireman's pole. A guttural groan flies from my lips. She starts to move, rolling her pelvis, and my hands grip on to her hips. I'm so familiar with every inch of her body, blindfolded, I could pick her out of a lineup of naked women. Worshipping her sensually curved body with my hands and mouth has become my favorite pastime. But her riding me, with her tits bouncing, mouth slack with pleasure and cheeks flushed pink with passion, is a close second.

As much as I want to pound upward into her, I let her have the reins, leaving control in her hands. Her pace quickens, and my fingers twitch on her hips as I resist the urge to grip and guide. She looks like a fucking goddess riding me with her long, black locks in wild disaray and her golden eyes hooded with desire. It's an image I'll never forget. She's my goddess, my religion, and my life.

SHE'S NESTLED on top of me while my fingertips trail up and down her spine. Her cheek is cushioned by my chest while my heart's steady rhythm drums beneath her ear.

I caress her cheek with my other hand. "Thank you for today."

"For going to your graduation or the sex?" She smiles.

"Both. But I think you know I was referring to the graduation. It meant so much more because you and our daughter were there to share it with me."

"You don't need to thank me for being there. I wouldn't have been anywhere else. I belong by your side and that's where I always want to be."

"Your support is what's gotten me through the last five years. Your unwavering belief that my dream of being an officer would come to fruition helped me make it through the times when I lost hope."

"Oh, Cord. No matter how many times I've told you that you're the one who made me believe in love again, I don't know if you truly believe it. You're the one who showed me what it means to be loved and cherished. You're the one who blessed me with a daughter."

My fingers trace along the elegant shape of her face. "You're the one who showed me I was worthy of being loved. I'm still not convinced I deserve you, but I'm sure as hell never letting you go."

She studies my face. "That's good to know because we're pregnant," she says, dropping a bombshell.

My eyebrows jump upward and my eyeballs bulge. “We are?”

She nods, her lips arching into a perfect smile.

I beam back at her, pulling her closer in my arms. “This day just keeps getting better. Jesus, what’s next?”

She rests her chin on my chest and looks up at me with amusement twinkling in her eyes. “We’re having twins.”

THE END

AFTERWORD

I hope you enjoyed our book, **That Boy**, which is part of the shared world of the All American Boy Series.

Want to read all of them? Find them all on Kindle Unlimited.
And thank you for leaving a review - it means the world to us.

The series includes the following books:

Sierra Hill The Boy Next Door
Poppy Parkes Boy Toy
Evan Grace The Boy Scout
Emily Robertson The Boyfriend Hoax
Kaylee Ryan and Lacey Black Boy Trouble
Kimberly Readnour Celebrity Playboy
Marika Ray Backroom Boy
Leslie McAdam Boy on a Train
KL Humphreys Bad Boy

Nicole Richard Hometown Boy
Remy Blake That Boy
Stephanie Browning The Boy She Left Behind
Stephanie Kay About a Boy
Renee Harless Lover Boy
SL Sterling Saviour Boy

PURCHASE THE WHOLE SERIES HERE

ABOUT THE AUTHOR

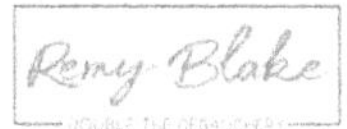

Remy Blake is a male and female author duo, Jacob Chance and Marley Valentine. Pairing up to have some fun, they write steamy, short reads, with insta love/lust, a guaranteed HEA. You can expect twice the debauchery in every book they write.

Facebook | Instagram | Twitter | Amazon Author Page | Goodreads Author Page | Book Bub

OTHER BOOKS BY REMY BLAKE

TEMPT
GUARDIAN | HUSBAND
CLIPPED | ROPED | TIMBER
DEBAUCHERY | THAT BOY

ACKNOWLEDGMENTS

Thank you to every reader who purchased, borrowed or read That Boy with Kindle Unlimited.

Thank you to Sierra Hill for organising this series and to all the other authors who we are so proud to be sharing this experience with. We had a blast.

Thank you to Shauna at Ink Machine Editing for all your hard work. We appreciate all the time you spend on our books, and for always fitting us into your schedule.

Thank you to all the members of both our reader groups, and all the new readers we've accumulated on the way. We're so appreciative of all your support, and we hope you stay with us for more Remy Blake books.

Until next time.

www.ingramcontent.com/pod-product-compliance
Ingram Content Group UK Ltd.
Pitfield, Milton Keynes, MK11 3LW, UK
UKHW021935190726
13853UKWH00004B/1466